'Sorry. I'll try again.'

She didn't dare look up into his eyes. Instead she stared straight ahead and tried with all her might to tie a proper bow tie.

'I...er...think you'll have to get someone else to do this,' she said, somewhat breathlessly.

When he didn't say a single word, she looked up, then desperately wished she hadn't. He was too close. Far, far too close.

His eyes searched hers with a harsh and haunted expression, betraying in that moment that he did still feel something for her.

'Why did you leave me?' he demanded angrily. 'Why, damn you?'

'Oh, Philip,' was all she could manage.

Mills & Boon Presents™ invites you to see how the other half marry in:

Society Weddings

They're gorgeous, they're glamorous... and they're getting married!

In this sensational five-book miniseries you'll be our VIP guests at some of the most talked-about weddings of the decade—spectacular events where the cream of society are gathered to celebrate the marriages of dazzling brides and grooms in equally breathtaking locations across the globe.

At each of these lavish ceremonies you'll meet some extra-special men and women—all rich, royal or just renowned!—whose stories are guaranteed to capture your imagination, your hearts...and the headlines! For in this sophisticated world of fame and fortune you can be sure of one thing: there'll be no end of scandal, surprises and passion!

We know you'll enjoy Miranda Lee's
THE WEDDING-NIGHT AFFAIR.

Next month, join us in a toast to
another happy couple in:
THE IMPATIENT GROOM
by Sara Wood

THE WEDDING-NIGHT AFFAIR

BY
MIRANDA LEE

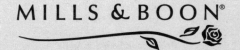

MILLS & BOON®

All the characters in this book have no existence outside the imagination of the author, and have no relation whatsoever to anyone bearing the same name or names. They are not even distantly inspired by any individual known or unknown to the author, and all the incidents are pure invention.

*First published in Great Britain 1999
Harlequin Mills & Boon Limited,
Eton House, 18-24 Paradise Road, Richmond, Surrey TW9 1SR*

© Miranda Lee 1999

ISBN 0 263 81776 8

*Set in Times Roman 10½ on 12 pt.
01-9909-47396 C1*

*Printed and bound in Spain
by Litografia Rosés, S.A., Barcelona*

CHAPTER ONE

THE door of Fiona's office burst open and Owen strode in, his round face pink with excitement. 'You've no idea who just rang and booked you for her son's wedding!' he exclaimed.

Fiona rolled her eyes, torn between exasperation and affection for her business partner. He was a dear man and a dear friend, hard-working and honest as the day was long. Mid-thirties, still a bachelor, and not at all gay as some people supposed, despite his penchant for pastel-coloured shirts and brightly coloured bow ties. Fiona thought the world of him.

He had this irritating habit, however, of accepting work on her behalf. Then he would race in to give her the details afterwards, and expect her to be thrilled to pieces.

She never was. She liked to vet all potential clients personally before accepting a job.

'You're right, Owen,' Fiona returned drily. 'I have no idea. How could I, since I didn't have the privilege of talking to this new client myself?'

As usual, Owen didn't look at all shame-faced. 'Couldn't, dear heart,' he countered breezily. 'You were on the phone when she rang, so Janey put the lady through to me.'

'Janey could have put the lady on hold for a while till I was free,' Fiona pointed out with mock sweetness.

Owen clamped a hand over his heart in horror at

5

such a suggestion. 'Put Mrs Kathryn Forsythe on hold? Good God, Fiona, she might have hung up!'

Fiona's own hand fluttered up to cover her own heart. 'Kathryn Forsythe?' she repeated weakly.

Owen beamed. 'I can see you're impressed. And so you should be! Do you have any idea what handling a Forsythe wedding will do for our business? Five-Star Weddings will be the toast of Sydney's social set! After everything goes off with your usual smooth and spectacular brilliance, Kathryn Forsythe will sing your praises to everyone who matters and there'll be a rush of society matrons banging on our doors to do their own daughter's wedding. Or son's, as is the case this time.'

Fiona's heart skipped another beat, before gradually returning to normal functions. What a fool she was to feel a thing after all this time—even shock!

'Well, well, well,' she mused aloud as she leant back in her black swivel chair and tapped her expertly manicured fingernails on the stainless steel armrests. 'So Philip's getting married at long last, is he?'

It was about time, she supposed. He would have been thirty last birthday. The perfect age for him to be finding a suitable bride and siring a suitable heir for his branch of the Forsythe fortune.

Owen looked slightly taken aback. 'You *know* Philip Forsythe?'

Fiona laughed a dry little laugh. '*Know* him! I was *married* to him once.' Briefly…

Owen dropped his rotund frame into one of the chairs she kept handy for clients. 'Good grief!' he gasped, then sagged, all his earlier enthusiasm swiftly abating. 'There goes our first high society gig.' Even his pink-spotted bow tie seemed to droop.

'Don't be silly. *You* can do it, can't you? Just say I'm all booked up.'

'That won't work,' Owen groaned. 'Mrs Forsythe wants the same co-ordinator who organised Craig Bateman's wedding.'

'Really? But that was hardly a society do. Just a cricketer and his childhood sweetheart. Very western suburbs, actually.'

'I know. But it was featured in one of the glossies, remember? It seems Mrs Forsythe was flipping through that particular issue at her hairdresser's and was most impressed by the photographs. The studio's name and number was printed underneath. Bill Babstock, if you recall. Anyway, when she rang to book Bill for her son's wedding, dear Bill very sensibly suggested she hire a professional wedding co-ordinator, then gave you the most glowing recommendation. When Mrs Forsythe rang just now, I did explain that you were very busy, but she promptly said that she'd heard you were the best and she wanted only the best for her son's wedding. So naturally I promised her you.'

'Naturally,' Fiona repeated in rueful tones.

Owen threw his hands up in the air. 'How was I to know you'd once been married to her infernal son? I mean…when I gave the woman your full name to jot down, she didn't react adversely. It was as though she didn't recognise it at all!'

Fiona thought about that for a moment. 'No, she wouldn't. Everyone called me Noni back then. And my surname was Stillman. Fiona Kirby wouldn't have meant a thing to her.'

Owen frowned. 'Kirby's not your maiden name?'

'No, it's my second husband's name.'

Owen gaped at her. '*Second* husband! Good grief, girl, I've known you six years, and whilst you've had more admirers than I've had bow ties you've never even got close to the altar. On top of that, you're only twenty-eight! Now I find you've got two husbands hidden in your past and the first belongs to one of Australia's richest families! Who was the other one? A famous brain surgeon? An international pop star?'

'No, a truck driver.'

'A truck driver!' he repeated disbelievingly.

'First name Kevin. Lived out at Leppington. Nice man, actually. I did him a favour when I divorced him, believe me.'

'And Philip Forsythe? Was he a nice man too?'

'Actually, yes, he was. Very.' She'd never held any real bitterness towards Philip. Or even Philip's father, who'd been surprisingly kind and gentle. It was his mother Fiona despised, his mother who'd looked down her nose at Noni and never given her brief marriage to Philip a chance.

'I suppose you did Philip Forsythe a favour when you divorced him too?' came her partner's caustic comment.

'How very perceptive of you, Owen. That's exactly what I did.' But it wasn't a divorce, she almost added. It was an annulment...

Fiona bit her tongue just in time. Such an announcement would lead to some sticky questions which she had no intention of answering.

'Let's face it, Owen,' she went on, 'I'm not good wife material. I like my own way far too much. I also hate to think we might lose this lucrative commission. Are you absolutely sure you can't convince Mrs

Forsythe to let you do it? Maybe we could say I'm ill.'

Owen sighed. 'I won't lie, Fiona. Lies always come back and bite you on the bum. Besides, I could hear the determination in her voice. She wants you for her son's wedding, and you alone.'

'That's a change,' Fiona muttered under her breath.

'What was that?'

Fiona looked up. 'I said that's a shame. As you said, this wedding would be worth a lot to us, both money-wise and reputation-wise.' She frowned and gnawed at her bottom lip. 'I wonder…'

Owen tried not to panic as he watched his partner's large brown eyes narrow into darkly determined slits. He knew that stubborn, focused look. When Fiona got the bit between the teeth, woe betide anyone who got in her way. Most times, Fiona's driven and obsessive personality didn't worry him. It was a plus, business-wise. She got things done.

This time, however, he feared getting things done might get things seriously *un*done.

'Oh, no, you don't!' he said, leaping out of the chair and jabbing a pudgy finger her way. 'Don't even *think* about it!'

'Think about what?'

'Trying to trick Kathryn Forsythe. I can see you now, putting on glasses and a blonde wig then waltz-ing in there with some funny accent, hoping your ex-mother-in-law won't recognise you.'

'But she won't recognise me, Owen,' Fiona said with blithe confidence. 'And I won't need to change a thing about my appearance. When Philip's mother knew me ten years ago I *was* a blonde. A ghastly straw colour done in a big mass of waves and curls. I also wore more make-up than a clown, carried twenty pounds too many and dressed like I was auditioning for a massage parlour. No top could be too tight; no skirt too short.'

Owen could only stare, first at the shoulder-length black hair which swung in a sleek, smooth, glossy curtain around his partner's striking but subtly made up face, then at the very slender body which was always displayed within a stylish but subtle outfit.

In appearance and dress, Fiona was the epitome of elegance and class, had been ever since he'd known her. The image she'd just painted of herself at the time of her marriage to Philip Forsythe certainly didn't match the woman she was today. Owen could not visualise her as some brassy voluptuous blonde bombshell.

Even if it was so—and he supposed it *was*—why would the likes of Philip Forsythe marry such a creature? He didn't know the man personally, but the bachelor sons of that particular family only ever married glamorous model-types, or the daughters of other equally rich families.

Unless, of course, it was for the sex.

Owen had to admit Fiona exuded a strong sexual allure which even *he* felt at times. Yet she wasn't his type at all. He fancied cuddly older women who laughed a lot, played a top game of Scrabble and cooked him casseroles. He never looked at a woman under forty, or a size fourteen.

Still, most men were madly attracted to Fiona. Once they slept with her, they became seriously smitten. She had dreadful trouble getting rid of her lovers after she tired of them.

And she always tired of them in the end.

Owen had often thought her a little cruel towards his sex, despite her always claiming that she never made a man any promises of permanency and had no idea why they presumed a deeper involvement than what was on offer. Perhaps the secret of that cruelty lay in those two marriages to those two supposedly 'nice' men.

'As for a funny accent,' Fiona was saying with a dismissive wave of her hand, 'I won't need to adopt one of those, either. The way I talk now is a lot different to the way I used to talk, believe me. I made Crocodile Dundee sound cultured back in those days. No, Owen, Mrs Forsythe won't recognise me. And Mr Forsythe senior won't have the chance. He passed away a couple of years back.'

'Did he? I didn't know that.'

'Cancer,' Fiona informed him. 'It didn't get all that much coverage in the papers. The funeral was private and closed to the public.'

There'd only been the one photo, Fiona recalled. That had been of Kathryn climbing into a big black car after the funeral was over. None of Philip.

Philip was not like his mother, or the rest of the Forsythes. He shunned publicity, and the media. Not once in the past ten years had Fiona ever caught a glimpse of him, either on television, or in the papers or magazines.

'And what was *he* like?' Owen asked.

'What?' Fiona looked up blankly. 'Who?'

'The groom's father,' Owen repeated drily.

'Actually…he was very nice.'

'Goodness, Fiona, your past seems peppered with very nice men. How is it, then, that down deep you're a man-hater?'

Fiona was startled for a moment, then defensive. 'That's a bit harsh, Owen, and not true at all. I love *you*, and you're a man.'

'I'm not talking about me, Fiona. I'm talking about the men you've dated, then discarded without so much as a backward glance. They thought you really cared for them but the truth is you just *used* them. That's not very nice, you know.'

Fiona stiffened for a moment, then shrugged. 'Sorry you think that, Owen, but they all knew the score. As for really caring for me, I doubt that very much. After an initial burst of pique at having their egos dented, they moved on to the next female swiftly enough. Now, let's get back to the subject at hand, which is that Kathryn Forsythe won't recognise me. Philip will be the only one who might. Though I stress the word *might*. Still, it's the mother who matters, isn't it? She's the one I'm meeting. Believe me when I assure you she won't know me from Adam.'

Owen stared at his partner and his friend and felt terribly sorry for her, because she *was* nice. Underneath all that delusionary and self-destructive bitterness, she was a genuine person, decent and kind, hard-working and generous. She cared about her clients and their worries. She always remembered everyone's birthday in the office, and was the softest touch when it came to charities. She never walked past one of those people selling useless badges and biros in the street, always stopping with a smile and a donation.

Goodness knows what had happened in those marriages of hers to make her hard where men were concerned, because she wasn't hard in any other department of her life. Determined, yes. And ambitious. But that was different. That was business.

Which reminded him. He had a business to protect here. He could not allow Fiona to carelessly endanger what they'd taken years to build together.

'We can't rely on Mrs Forsythe not recognising you, Fiona,' Owen said firmly. 'If you don't reveal who you are up front and it comes out later, then she's going to be furious and your name will be mud. Which means *our* name will be mud. I see no other solution than for you to keep the appointment I made for you, confess your identity with tact and diplomacy, then offer her my services once again. At least that way, even if she decides against using Five-Star Weddings, she won't be inclined to blacken our name.'

Fiona leant back even further in her chair and mulled over Owen's suggestion. It made sound business sense, she supposed. And she would still have the satisfaction of seeing Kathryn Forsythe's face when she revealed her true identity.

In a way, it would be *better* than tricking her, showing the hateful woman in person that the one-time object of her snobbish scorn was no longer as ignorant as sin and as common as muck. Philip's derided and despised first wife could pass muster in the best of circles these days!

Fiona now knew how to dress, how to talk and how to act on whatever occasion was thrown at her. She owned a half-share in a blossoming business, a beautiful flat overlooking Lavender Bay, and a wardrobe full of designer clothes. She had a vast knowledge of food and wine. She had an appreciation of art and music of all kinds. She could even ski!

But, best of all, she could have just about any man she wanted, if and when she wanted them, for as little or as long as she wanted them.

For a moment Fiona wondered ruefully what would happen if she ran into Philip again. *Would* he recognise her? If he did, what would he think of Fiona as compared to Noni? Would he want *Fiona* as he'd once wanted *Noni*?

It was an intriguing speculation.

As much as she was over her love for Philip at long last, she still felt an understandable curiosity about the man. What did he look like now? And what was the woman like he'd finally decided to marry?

'Very well, Owen,' she agreed, and snapped forward in her chair. 'I'll go and throw myself on Mrs Forsythe's mercy. But first, do tell. Why is it Kathryn's job to organise her son's wedding? Doesn't the lucky bride *have* a mother?'

Owen shrugged. 'Apparently not.'

'So who is this undoubtedly beautiful and well-brought-up creature who's to be welcomed into the bosom of the Forsythe family?'

'I have no idea. We didn't get that far.'

'So when's the appointment for?'

'Tomorrow morning at ten.'

'On a *Saturday*? You know I never see anyone on a Saturday! For pity's sake, Owen, I have a wedding on tomorrow afternoon.'

'Rebecca can handle it.'

'No,' Fiona said sharply. 'She's not ready.'

'Yes, she is. You've trained her very well, Fiona. You just don't like delegating. Much as I admire your dedication and perfectionism, the time has come to give Rebecca some added responsibility.'

'Maybe,' Fiona said, 'but not this time. The bride's mother is expecting *me*. I refuse to let her down on such an important day.'

'Maybe you could do both,' Owen suggested hopefully. 'The appointment *and* the wedding.'

'I doubt it, not if Mrs Forsythe still lives way out at Kenthurst, which by the look on your face she does. That's a good hour's drive through traffic from my place, and far too far from tomorrow's wedding down at Cronulla. You'll have to ring back and change the appointment to Sunday, Owen. Make it for eleven. I'm not getting up early on a Sunday morning for the likes of her.'

'But…but…'

'Just do it, Owen. Tell the woman the truth: that Fiona has a wedding to organise tomorrow and can't make it. She'll probably admire my…what was it you said?…my dedication and perfectionism?'

Owen groaned. 'You're a hard woman.'

'Don't be silly. I'm as soft as butter.'

'Yeah, straight out of the freezer.'

'Trust me, Owen, I know what I'm doing. The Forsythes of this world have more respect for people who don't chase or grovel. Be polite, but firm. I'll bet it works a charm.'

It did, to Owen's surprise. 'She was only too accommodating about it all,' he relayed ten minutes later, still startled. 'And she wants you to stay for Sunday lunch. Fortunately for us, her son and his bride-to-be can't make it that day. Thank heavens for that, I say. And thank heavens the groom doesn't live at home.'

Fiona already knew Philip didn't live at home. The phone book had been very informative of his whereabouts over the years. There weren't too many P. Z. Forsythes in this world, and only one in Sydney. Fifteen months after they'd broken up—around the time he would have finished his law degree—he'd bobbed up at an address in Paddington, only a hop, step and a jump from the city.

The following year he'd moved further out to Bondi. More recently he'd moved again, to an even more salubrious address at Balmoral Beach, which, though over the bridge on the north side, still wasn't far from town.

Back in his Paddington days, Fiona had used to regularly ring him, just so she could hear his voice, hanging up after he answered. Once, not long after his move to Bondi, she'd rung him on a Saturday night and pretended to be wanting someone called Nigel, just so she could extend the conversation for a few seconds, then had got the shock of her life when Philip called out to some Nigel person.

'He'll be with you in a sec, honey,' Philip had said, before putting the phone down. The sounds of a party in the background had been crushingly clear. Laughter. Music. Gaiety.

Fiona had hurriedly hung up and vowed never to do that again.

And she hadn't. She had, however, never got out of the habit of checking Philip's address every time a new phone directory arrived, which was how she knew about his move to Balmoral.

Fiona glanced up from her thoughts to find her partner frowning down at her. She smiled up at him. A rather sardonic smile, but a smile all the same. 'Stop looking so worried, Owen.'

'I want to know how you're going to handle telling Mrs Forsythe the truth about yourself.'

'With kid gloves, I assure you. I *can* be tactful and diplomatic, you know. I can even be sweet and charming when I want to be. Don't I always have the mother of the bride eating out of my hand?'

'Yeah. But Mrs Forsythe isn't the mother of the bride. She's the mother of the groom, and *you're* the groom's first wife!'

CHAPTER TWO

FIONA pulled over to the kerb and consulted the street directory one more time to make sure she knew the way to Kenthurst. She'd gone there only twice, after all, ten years before.

Kenthurst was not a suburb one passed through by accident, or on the way to somewhere. It was more of an 'invitation only' address.

A semi-rural and increasingly exclusive area on the northern outskirts of Sydney, Kenthurst boasted picturesque countryside with lots of trees, undulating hills and fresh air. The perfect setting for secluded properties owned by privileged people who liked peace and privacy.

Wealthy Sydney businessmen had once built summer houses up in the Blue Mountains or down in the southern highlands to escape the heat and the rat-race of the city. Now they were more inclined to build air-conditioned palaces on five to twenty-five acres out Kenthurst or Dural way, and live there most of the time.

Philip's father had done just that, though he'd also owned a huge Double Bay apartment where he'd stayed overnight when business kept him late in town, or when he'd taken his wife to the theatre or the opera. It was an enormous place, covering the whole floor of a solid pre-war three-storeyed building, lavishly furnished with antiques, and with a four-poster bed in the main bedroom which had belonged to a French countess. Fiona knew this for a fact because she'd slept in it.

Well…not exactly *slept*.

She wondered if Philip had ever 'slept' with his bride-to-be in that same bed, if he'd taken her to the same mindless raptures he'd taken her own silly self.

Now, now, don't go getting all bitter and twisted, she lectured herself sharply. Waste of time, honey. Concentrate on the job at hand, which is getting to Kathryn's house by eleven.

Fiona didn't want to be late. She didn't want to give the woman the slightest excuse for looking down her nose at her again.

Gritting her teeth, Fiona bent her head to concentrate on the directory. Once the various street turnings were memorised, she angled her freshly washed and polished Audi away from the kerb and back onto the highway.

A small wry smile lifted the corner of her mouth as she drove on. The car wasn't the only thing that had been washed and polished to perfection that morning, mocking her claim that she would not get up early on a Sunday for the likes of Kathryn Forsythe.

Pride had had her up at six. By nine there hadn't been an inch of her body which wasn't attended to, from the top of her sleekly groomed head to her perfectly pedicured toenails. Fiona had told herself that even if there was only the remotest chance of having to remove her shoes and stockings—or any other part of her clothing—she was going to be as perfect *underneath* as she was on the surface.

Oddly enough, it had been the surface clothes which had ended up causing her the most trouble. Downright perverse, in Fiona's opinion, when she had a wardrobe chock-full of the best clothes money could buy.

The fact that it was winter should have made the choice of outfit easier. But it hadn't. The black suits she favoured for work had seemed too funereal, her grey outfits a little washed out, now that her summer tan had long faded. Chocolate-brown and camel were last year's colours. She certainly wasn't going to show up in *them*! Which had left cream or taupe. Fiona never wore loud colours. Or white.

Certainly not white, had come the bitter thought.

She had dithered till a decision had simply *had* to be made. Time was beginning to run out.

In desperation, she'd settled on a three-piece trouser-suit in a lightweight cream wool. It had straight-leg trousers, a V-necked waistcoat and a long-sleeved lapelled jacket. The buttons on the waistcoat were covered, but rimmed in gold, so a necklace would have been overdone for daytime.

But she had slipped eighteen carat gold earrings into her pierced ears and a classically styled gold watch onto her wrist—both gifts from one-time admirers. Her shoes and bag were tan, and made of the softest leather. They'd cost a small fortune. Make-up had been kept to a minimum, her mouth and nails a subtle brown. Her perfume was another gift from an admirer, who'd said it was as exotic and sensual as she was.

Finally, she'd been fairly satisfied with her appearance, and just before ten had left her flat, ready to face the woman who'd almost destroyed her.

'But I rose again, Kathryn,' Fiona said aloud as she turned off the highway and headed for Kenthurst. 'Just like the phoenix.'

Fiona laughed, well aware that the likes of Noni

would not even have known what the phoenix was. 'You've come a long way, honey,' she complimented herself. 'A long, long way. Worth a few nerves to show Philip's darling mama just how far!'

The sun broke through the clouds at that point, bouncing off the shiny polished surfaces of the silver car and into her eyes. Fiona reached for the designer sunglasses which she kept tucked in the car door pocket, slipped them on, and smiled.

Fifteen minutes later she was driving slowly past the Forsythe place, her confident smile long replaced by a puzzled frown.

It had changed in ten years. And she wasn't talking about the high brick wall which now surrounded the property. Somehow, it looked smaller than she remembered, and less intimidating. Yet it was still a mansion; still very stately, with its imitation Georgian façade; still perched up on a hill high enough to have an un-interrupted three-hundred-and-sixty-degree view of the surrounding countryside.

Fiona stopped the car, stared hard at the house, then slowly nodded up and down. Of course! How silly of her! It wasn't the house which had changed but herself, and her perceptions. After all, she was no stranger to mansions these days, and no longer overawed by the evidence of wealth.

Her confident smile restored, Fiona swung the Audi around and returned to the driveway, where the iron gates were already open, despite the security camera on top of the gatepost and an intercom system built into the cement postbox.

It seemed careless to leave the gates open, but per-haps Kathryn had opened them in readiness for her arrival. Her watch did show two minutes to eleven.

Fiona drove on through, a glance in the rear-vision mirror revealing that the gates remained open behind her.

Oh, well. She shrugged. Kathryn Forsythe's security wasn't *her* problem, but it seemed silly to go to the trouble and expense of having all that put in without using it. Such rich remote properties would be a target for break-ins and burglaries. Maybe even kidnappings. You couldn't be too careful these days.

Admittedly, Philip's branch of the family wasn't as high-profile as his two uncles'. His uncle Harold was a captain of industry, owning several food and manufacturing companies as well as a string of racehorses, whilst his uncle Arnold was a major player in the media and hotels, along with expensive hobbies such as polo and wine.

Philip's father, Malcolm, had been the youngest of the three Forsythe boys and had gone into corporate law, the law firm he'd established handling all the legal transactions for his older brothers' business dealings. Philip had once told her that his father was probably richer than his two brothers, because he didn't waste money on gambling and other women.

All three Forsythe brothers had married beautiful girls from well-to-do society families, thereby increasing their wealth and securing a good gene pool for their children. Harold had sired a mixed brood of five children, and Arnold three strapping sons. Malcolm had only had the one child, Philip.

Surprisingly, none of the brothers had ever divorced, despite rumours of serious philandering by Harold and Arnold. All three Forsythe wives were regularly photographed by the Sunday papers and gossip magazines, showing off their tooth-capped smiles along with their latest face-lifts. They seemed to spend half their lives at fashion shows, charity balls and racing carnivals.

Fiona had once been impressed by it all.

Not any more, however.

Her brown eyes were cool as they swept over the groomed lawns and perfectly positioned trees, her pulse not beating one jot faster as she drew closer to the house. A little different from the first time she'd come up this driveway, her heart pounding like a jackhammer, her stomach in sickening knots. Back then she'd been as nervous as the heroine in *Rebecca*, driving up to Manderley with her wealthy new husband at her side.

Fiona could well understand that poor young bride's feelings of inadequacy and insecurity. She'd felt exactly the same way back then. Ironic that on *her* unexpected return to Manderley *she* was now the first wife.

The house grew larger on approach. But of course it *was* large. Wide, white and two-storeyed, with a huge pitched grey slate roof and long, tall, symmetrically placed windows. It looked English in design, and somewhat in setting, with its clumps of English trees and ordered gardens. Nothing, however, could disguise the Australian-ness of the bright clear blue sky, or the mountains in the distance, also blue with the haze from the millions of eucalypti which covered them.

The tarred and winding driveway finally gave way to a more formal circular section, with a red gravel surface and a Versailles-like fountain in the middle. The Audi crunched to a halt in front of the white-columned portico and almost immediately the front door opened and the lady of the house stepped out into the sunshine.

Fiona frowned as she stared over at Philip's mother.

Kathryn was still as superbly groomed as she remembered. And just as elegant, in a royal blue woollen dress, with pearls at her throat and not a blonde hair out of place.

But she looked older. *Much* older. Probably even around her real age.

She had to be coming up for sixty, Fiona supposed. Ten years ago she'd been in her late forties, though she'd looked no more than thirty-five.

She appeared frail as well now, as though the stuffing had been knocked out of her. There was a slight stoop about her shoulders and a sadness in her face which struck an annoyingly sympathetic chord in Fiona.

Her whole insides revolted at this unlikely response. *Sympathy for Kathryn Forsythe? Never!*

Steeling herself against such a heresy, Fiona pulled the keys out of the ignition, practically threw them in her handbag, climbed out and swung the door shut. Sweeping off her sunglasses, she turned to face her one-time enemy, waiting coolly to be appraised and *not* recognised.

Kathryn's lovely but faded blue eyes *did* sweep slowly over her from head to toe, but, as Fiona had predicted to Owen, there was not a hint of recognition, let alone rejection. Nothing but acceptance and approval. One could even go so far as to say…admiration.

Oddly, this did not give Fiona the satisfaction she'd hoped for. She didn't feel triumphant at all. Suddenly, she felt mean and underhand.

'You must be Fiona,' Kathryn said in a softly gentle voice, smiling warmly as she came forward and held out a welcoming hand.

Fiona found herself totally disarmed, smiling stiffly back and taking the offered hand while her mind fairly whirled. She's only being nice to you because you *look* the way you do, she warned herself. Don't ever think this woman has really changed, not down deep, where it matters. She's still a terrible snob. If she ever found out who you really were, she'd cut you dead, and, yes, she'd be furious. Make no mistake about that. So put on a good act here, darling heart, make your abject apologies and get the hell out of Manderley!

'And you must be Mrs Forsythe,' she returned in her now well-educated voice, a far cry from the rough Aussie drawl she'd once used, with slang and the odd swear-word thrown in for good measure.

'Not to you, my dear. You must call me Kathryn.' Philip's mother actually linked arms with her, gathering her to her side and giving her a little squeeze.

Fiona froze. The Kathryn Forsythe of ten years before would never have done such a thing, not even to her friends and relatives. Philip's mother had been a reserved and distant woman with an aversion to touching.

'After all,' Kathryn went on, before Fiona could recover from her shock to form a single word, 'we're going to be spending a lot of time together over the next few weeks, aren't we?'

Fiona should have put her right then and there, but she hesitated too long and the moment was lost.

'So how did your wedding go yesterday, dear?' Kathryn asked as she steered Fiona over towards the house. 'You had lovely weather for it, considering it's August.'

'It…um…it went very well,' Fiona replied truthfully, while she tried to work out how to tactfully escape this increasingly awkward situation.

'I can imagine everything you do goes very well, my dear,' Kathryn complimented her. 'I'm already impressed with your punctuality and your appearance. A lot of people these days don't seem to care how late they are for an appointment, or how they look when they get there. I've always felt that clothes reveal a lot about a man, and everything about a woman. You and I are going to get along very well, my dear. Very well indeed.'

Now *that* sounded more like the old Kathryn, Fiona thought.

To be strictly honest, however, she now shared some of those sentiments. She couldn't abide people who were late for business appointments. Neither was she impressed with the slovenly dressed, or the grunge brigade. Fiona had found that people who didn't care about their own appearance were usually not much good at their jobs.

You mean you judge a book by its cover these days, darling? an annoying inner voice pointed out drily.

The sound of a car speeding up the driveway interrupted her distracting train of thought.

'That will be my son,' Kathryn said, just as a black Jaguar with tinted windows roared into view. It braked hard inches before the gravel section, then passed sedately by them before purring to a cat-like halt on the other side of her Audi.

Panic had Fiona jamming her sunglasses back over

her suddenly terrified eyes and praying Philip wouldn't recognise her with them on.

'I thought you said Phi...your son...couldn't come today,' she pronounced tautly.

Fortunately, Kathryn didn't seem to notice her agitation. 'He rang a while back on his mobile to say that Corinne—she's his fiancée—had woken with a migraine this morning and begged off going on the harbour cruise luncheon they were supposed to attend. He didn't fancy going alone so decided to pop home for lunch instead. He rang off before I could remind him you would be here as well.'

Fiona found herself staring over at the car. From the side, she couldn't see the driver, because of the tinted windows. Several fraught seconds ticked away without Philip making an appearance, and she found herself waiting breathlessly for that moment when the driver's door would open.

Fiona began to feel sick to her stomach. It had been a dreadful mistake coming here today, she was beginning to realise. A dreadful, dreadful mistake!

As though in slow motion, the door finally opened and his dark head came into view, followed by his shoulders—his very broad shoulders. Once fully upright, he turned to glance at them over the bonnet of the car.

Was she imagining it or was he staring at her?

Surely not. She *had* to be imagining it. He couldn't have recognised her, not with her sunglasses on!

She was being paranoid. Besides, he was wearing sunglasses too. Impossible to see where his eyes were being directed, or to determine their expression with those masking shades on.

Which was a reassuring factor from her own point

of view, because the moment he strode round the front of his car and started towards them Fiona's eyes began eating him up in exactly the same way they had the very first day he'd walked into Gino's fish and chip shop ten years before.

Yet he was only wearing jeans and a grey sweater. Nothing fancy. Just casual clothes.

Philip the man, she was forced to accept, was even more impressive than Philip the youth, the promise of future perfection now fulfilled. His long, lanky frame was all filled out, his once boyishly handsome face fined down to a more mature and classical handsomeness, his thick unruly brown hair now elegantly tamed and groomed.

At twenty, Philip had been dishy.

At thirty, he was downright dangerous.

Kathryn disengaged her arm from Fiona's as Philip approached, moving forward to give her son an astonishing hug. 'It's so nice to see you, son. I hope you didn't drive too fast, now.'

'I never drive too fast, Mother dearest. Can't afford to get any blemishes on my record.'

'My son's a lawyer,' his mother proudly explained, with a smiling glance over her shoulder at Fiona.

Philip's gaze swung to Fiona as well, who felt as if there was a vice around her chest, squeezing tightly.

'So, who have we here, Mother?' he said quite nonchalantly. 'Aren't you going to introduce us?'

A little of the pressure eased, though a perverse dismay was added to the emotions besieging Fiona at that moment. So he *hadn't* recognised her! She shouldn't have been disappointed. But, stupidly, she was. He'd once claimed he would never forget her, that he would love her till the end of time.

'The end of time' apparently expired after ten years, came the pained thought. If truth be told, it had probably begun to run out the moment she'd exited his life.

Philip's father had been so right about his son's so-called love. It had had about as much substance as fairy-floss.

'Your memory for some things is appalling these days, Philip,' his mother said, blissfully unaware of the irony within those words. 'Fiona is the wedding co-ordinator from Five-Star Weddings that I was telling you about on Friday. I'm sure I mentioned I was having lunch with her today. Fiona, this is Philip, the absent-minded groom. Philip, this is Fiona. Fiona Kirby, wasn't it, dear?'

'Yes, that's right.'

'How do you do, Mrs Kirby?' he greeted her.

'Miss,' she corrected sharply, and his eyebrows lifted above the sunglasses.

'My mistake. Sorry. Ms Kirby.'

'Oh, don't call her that, Philip,' his mother said with a soft laugh. 'We're already on a first-name basis, aren't we, my dear? As I said to Fiona, we'll be spending quite a deal of time together in the near future so we might as well be friends.'

Fiona wanted to scream and make a dash for the car. *Friends?* She was no more capable of being friends with Philip and his mother than she was of being friends with a pair of serial killers.

Yet for the moment she was trapped. Owen would kill her if she alienated such an influential family as the Forsythes, thereby damaging the reputation of Five-Star Weddings. And, frankly, she wouldn't blame him. She'd been very foolish indeed to come here in person and risk all for the sake of her infernal pride.

'You've already decided on Five-Star Weddings to do the wedding?' Philip asked his mother, a frown bunching his forehead.

'I certainly have. The moment I met Fiona I knew she was the right person to do the job.'

'Did you indeed? How interesting. I, however, would like to see what she has in mind before any decisions are made and any contracts signed.'

'Lawyers!' Kathryn exclaimed, with a roll of her eyes and an apologetic glance towards Fiona. 'They see trouble at every turn.'

'Not at all,' Philip countered smoothly. 'I simply don't believe in rushing into anything, especially when it comes to business dealings. The world is full of con-artists and shysters. I know nothing of Five-Star Weddings other than what you told me over the phone. And absolutely nothing about Ms Kirby here, except what I can see for myself. As attractive as her outer package might be, in reality she might be anybody!'

Fiona stiffened, then saw red. Be damned with what Owen thought. Be damned with everything. She was not going to let Philip stand there and insult her.

Sweeping off her sunglasses, she glared up at him, her cold fury only increasing when he *still* didn't recognise her.

'Five-Star Weddings has an impeccable record and reputation, Mr Forsythe,' she stated through clenched teeth. 'As do I. Might I remind you that your mother solicited this appointment, not the other way around? Nevertheless, I can show you many personal letters of recommendation, plus extensive portfolios of weddings I have arranged. Believe it or not, I am heavily booked at the moment, and only came here as a favour for my business partner, who agreed to this appointment without consulting me.

'Under the circumstances, it would be better if you found someone else, Kathryn,' she directed at Philip's mother. 'Lovely to have met you.'

Kathryn grabbed her arm before she could make good her escape. 'Please, don't go!' she cried, before rounding on her son, her voice trembling and full of reproach. 'What on earth's got into you, Philip? I've never known you be so rude before!'

'I wasn't being rude. I was trying to be sensible. Anyway, given that Ms Kirby says she overbooked, it's better you *do* hire someone else.'

'But I don't *want* someone else! I want Fiona. She's the one who was recommended. On top of that, I *like* her. You'd do the job personally, wouldn't you, dear, if I paid you double your usual fee?'

'Well, I… I…'

'Mother, for pity's sake, you don—'

'Philip!' his mother interrupted sternly, the stubborn and autocratic Kathryn of ten years ago emerging for a few moments. 'You and Corinne asked me to organise your wedding and I am only too happy to do so. But with your proposed wedding date only ten weeks off, and your bride-to-be overseas for most of that time, I will need help. I want Fiona to be that help. Please don't be difficult about this.'

Philip stood there silently for several tense seconds, his shoulders squared, his mouth grim.

Fiona didn't know whether to laugh or cry. It really was a bizarre situation.

Suddenly, Philip swept off his sunglasses and stared deep into her eyes, his own no longer masked.

They had always been his most attractive feature, his eyes. A vivid blue and deeply set, with a dark rim around the iris which gave them an added intensity, both of colour and expression. The first time he'd looked at her all those years ago, across the shop counter, her knees had gone to jelly.

He stared at her now and she stared boldly back, her knees only marginally shaky.

His gaze raked her face, his expression puzzled and searching. For what? she thought angrily. Was he finally being bothered by a faint glimmer of familiarity? Was his subconscious teasing him with all those times he'd looked deeply into her eyes and told her she was the most incredible, adorable, irresistible girl in the world?

Quite abruptly, his eyes cooled to a bland, infuriatingly unreadable expression.

'I apologise,' he said, but insincerely, she believed. 'I didn't mean to cast aspersions on your reputation. I have to confess to a certain cynicism these days, especially in matters of business. I'm sure Five-Star Weddings is without peer in its field and I'm sure you're one of its star co-ordinators.'

'She certainly is,' his mother joined in, looking both relieved and pleased. 'You should have heard the photographer rave. He said Fiona was the very best in the business.'

'I'm sure,' Philip murmured. 'Still, perhaps Fiona could humour me a little by coming inside and telling us some more about herself. But first, I'm dying for some decent coffee, Mother dearest. Do you think you could make me some? I know it's Brenda's day off, but you make much better coffee than she does anyway.'

'Flatterer!' Kathryn returned, but she was beaming.

'What about you, Fiona?' Philip said, with the sort of suave smoothness she both desired and despised in a man. 'You look like a coffee girl to me.'

'Coffee would be nice,' she agreed, with a smooth smile of her own. She would have liked to tell him where to shove his coffee, but things had moved beyond her making any further fuss, or flouncing off in some dramatic exit. She had to see this unfortunate scenario through now, or Owen would kill her! But come tomorrow she was going to fall mysteriously ill and be unable to take on any new clients.

'I'll take Fiona through to the terrace,' Philip informed his mother.

'Oh, yes, do,' she replied. 'It's lovely out there today. I won't be long.'

Kathryn hurried off to do her son's bidding. Another vast change in the woman's character. She'd never been sweet and accommodating in the past. She'd expected everyone else to do *her* bidding.

'This way,' Philip murmured, taking Fiona's elbow rather forcefully and steering her speedily inside, across the spacious marble foyer and down the wide cool hallway which bisected the bottom floor of the house.

Fiona barely had time to scoop in a couple of steadying breaths before she was ushered through a pair of white French doors onto an enormous sun-drenched terrace which stretched the length of the house.

It was an area she'd never been, or seen before. Probably new, she decided.

As Philip directed her towards the closest grouping of outdoor furniture Fiona replaced her sunglasses and glanced around, her wedding co-ordinator's eye automatically taking over. Kathryn wouldn't need to book a special place for the reception, she realised. This setting could look magnificent, with the right kind of marquee and the right lighting.

There wasn't just the one terrace. There were two. The top one conveniently had shelter, with a pergola-style roof which had slats one could open or shut. The next terrace, much longer and wider than the first, was tiled in terracotta and incorporated a large rectangular swimming pool, lined at each end by Corinthian columns of grey marble. It reminded Fiona of a photograph she'd once seen of a pool in ancient Rome. All that was missing was the nude statues.

At each end of the terraces lay an extensive garden, which was distinctly tropical, full of ferns and palms and rich green shrubs of all kinds. Oddly, it didn't look out of place, exuding an exotic and sensual pull on the senses, making one long for the warm, balmy evenings of summer.

Fiona could easily envisage a near-naked Philip, stretched out along the edge of the pool, his eyes shut, one hand languidly trailing through the cool blue water. She could almost feel the coolness of that water on her heated skin as she imagined swimming towards him, stopping right next to him, then taking that wickedly idle hand and lifting it to her hot…wet…flesh.

Philip scraping out a chair for her on the flagstones snapped Fiona out of her erotic daydream with the abruptness of a drowning man gasping to the surface. Disorientated for a moment, she found herself staring down at the strong male hands gripping the back of the white wrought-iron chair and remembering how good he was with those hands, how well they had known her body and how completely they had been able to coerce her to his will.

Surely they couldn't *still* do that, she thought, then panicked as her body experienced a deep and violent burst of desire.

Self-disgust followed, but a fraction too late in her opinion. Clenching her teeth, Fiona wrenched her eyes away from those offending hands and swiftly sat down. She didn't watch Philip stride round to select the chair directly opposite, not looking back at him till he was seated.

'Right,' he said, his voice cut and dried as he slid his sunglasses back on. 'Now, let's stop all this pretence, Noni. What in hell are you up to?'

CHAPTER THREE

'OH!' FIONA gasped, sitting up straight. 'You *did* recognise me.'

'Keep it down, for pity's sake,' he hissed. 'I don't want my mother to hear any of this. And, yes, of course I recognised you. How could you possibly imagine I wouldn't? I knew it was you the moment I drove up. You weren't quite quick enough putting on those sunglasses. Still, I can understand why my mother didn't twig. That's some make-over, Noni. Most impressive. But back to the point. What are you up to? Why this sick little charade?'

Any momentary elation Fiona had felt at Philip's having recognised her quickly faded at his sarcastic and accusing tone. She automatically moved back into survival mode.

'I'm not up to anything,' she defended coolly. 'It's exactly as I said earlier. My business partner made this appointment with your mother without my knowledge. I tried to get out of it. I explained to Owen that you and I had been married briefly years ago, and that I couldn't possibly do your wedding, but he still insisted I show up today in person. He said the future of Five-Star Weddings was at stake. He wanted me to apologise and recommend him instead, but when Kathryn didn't recognise me I hesitated too long, and then you showed up unexpectedly and…well…' She shrugged.

'Things got even more complicated,' Philip finished drily.

'Yes,' Fiona agreed.

There was a short, sharp silence while he just stared at her.

'You must have suspected my mother wouldn't recognise you,' he said curtly, 'looking as you look today.'

'It did briefly cross my mind.'

He laughed. 'More than briefly, I'll warrant. So...did you enjoy fooling her? Did you get a kick out of it?'

She contemplated lying, but couldn't see any point. 'I thought I would,' she confessed ruefully.

He frowned. 'But you didn't?'

'No,' she confessed, still a little confused by her reaction to his mother. 'No, I didn't. She's not the same woman I remember, Philip. Somehow, I couldn't find it in my heart to hold any more malice towards her.'

His frown deepened. 'What do you mean...malice?'

'Oh, Philip, don't pretend you don't know what she did all those years ago, how she made me feel.'

'I know she made things difficult for you. But, believe me, she would have made things difficult for any girl I wanted to marry back then. The bottom line is it wasn't my mother who ended our marriage, Noni. It was you.'

She opened her mouth to defend what she'd done, then stopped herself. Once again, she couldn't see the point. It was over. Philip was getting married again. No doubt to some rich, beautiful girl he loved to death and of whom his mother heartily approved.

As for herself. Well...she had her career.

'I was very young,' Fiona said flatly. 'So were you. We were from two different worlds. Our marriage would never have worked. I did the right thing.' She looked away from him then, afraid that she might do something appalling like burst into tears.

When she looked back, several seconds later, she was once again under control. 'What's done is done,' she stated brusquely. 'Let's not hash over ancient history, Philip. Just tell me what you want me to do about your mother and your wedding.'

He didn't answer her straight away, considering her at length from behind his sunglasses till her irritation table rose to dangerous levels.

'Will you be in trouble with your partner if you lose this job?' he finally asked.

'Probably,' she snapped.

'Then do it.'

Fiona automatically shrank from the idea.

'Come now, Noni, it's no big deal. It's not as though we mean anything to each other any more,' he said dismissively. 'As you just said, our marriage—such as it was—is ancient history. We don't have to tell anyone who you really are. I've never told Corinne about you, and Mother will never recognise you. On top of that, you've been offered double your usual fee. You'd be a fool to knock it back.'

His cold pragmatism put her mind—and her emotions—back on track. He was right, of course. She'd be a fool to say no. And she was no longer a fool, either over money or men.

'You'll have to practise calling me Fiona,' she pointed out drily.

'No trouble. Fiona suits you better these days, anyway.'

Fiona gritted her teeth. 'And you'll have to practise not being sarcastic.'

'I wasn't being sarcastic. I was just saying it as it was.'

Fiona bristled. 'You don't like the way I look?'

'Does it matter what *I* like? My mother thinks you're the ant's pants. That must give you great satisfaction.'

'It does, actually.'

'Then that's all that matters. She's the one you'll be working with most of the time. The groom has very little to do with wedding preparations.'

'True.' She'd *never* agree otherwise.

'Of course I *am* a little curious as to how you achieved this stunning transformation, and how you came to be a partner in a highly successful business. The last I heard of you, you were married to some truck driver.'

Fiona's mouth dropped open. 'How…how did you know about that?'

His mouth smiled, but his eyes remained a mystery behind those increasingly irritating sunglasses. Yet, at the same time, she was grateful for her own.

'Curiosity sent me looking for you after I finished university,' he explained. 'I didn't find you but I did find your father. He seemed happy to tell me about your marriage to a trucking mate of his, a man named Kevin Kirby. That's why I called you Mrs Kirby when we were introduced just now. But you soon put me straight about that! Since you're a little young to be a widow, I gather there was a divorce?'

'You gather right.'

'Your decision again, Fiona?'

'It was, actually.'

'What went wrong?' he asked. 'You certainly

couldn't say you were from two different worlds on that occasion.'

'No. I certainly couldn't,' she returned, her voice as hard as her heart. 'The bare truth is that Kevin wanted me to stay home and have children, and I didn't. Our divorce was quite amicable. He's now married again with a couple of kids.'

'And you're on your way to your first million,' he mocked.

'And what's wrong with that?' she snapped.

'Nothing, I guess. If that's all you want out of life. *Is* that all you want nowadays, Fiona? Money?'

'A little respect goes down well. But money's good. The money I earn for myself, that is.'

'Ahh. A truly independent woman. Very admirable. I dare say you live alone these days?'

'I do.'

'But you date, of course. Celibacy would not be your strong point.'

'Nor yours, Philip,' she shot back at him.

He laughed. '*Touché*. So, are you sleeping with this business partner of yours? What was his name? Owen something or other?'

'I have no intention of answering any questions about my personal life,' came her cool reply.

'You're not asking Fiona impertinent questions, are you, son?' Kathryn said wearily as she seemed to materialise beside Fiona's shoulder, bending to slide a tray onto the table. It held an elegant white coffee pot with three equally elegant white coffee mugs surrounding it. A matching jug held cream, no doubt, and the crystal sugar bowl sparkled in the sun.

'Don't take any notice of him, dear,' Kathryn went on as she sat down between them. 'Once a lawyer, always a lawyer. They like giving people the third degree, even innocent ones. I sometimes feel sorry for the witnesses Philip cross-examines.'

'You're a *criminal* lawyer?' Fiona exclaimed, taken aback. She'd presumed he'd gone into corporate law, in his father's company. That had certainly been his father's plan for him.

'Philip's beginning to make a name for himself in court, aren't you, dear?' his mother said proudly.

'I've had some modest successes recently.'

Kathryn laughed softly. 'Now who's being modest? How do you take your coffee, Fiona?'

'Oh…um…white, with one sugar, please,' she answered, a little distractedly, almost adding 'the same as Philip.' Goodness, she was a mess!

'Just to put your mind at rest, Mother,' Philip said casually while Kathryn was pouring the coffee. 'It's perfectly all right by me for Fiona to do the wedding. Now that I've had a chance to talk to her, I'm more than impressed with her credentials, but especially her professional attitude. I recognise a high achiever when I hear one. I'm sure she'll do a top job. As for her fee, and the contract, I'll take care of that personally. You live too far out of town to be bothered with that. I presume you have an office somewhere in the city, Fiona? Perhaps a business card as well?'

Fiona hated the thought of him dropping in to the office, but what could she do? She could hardly say as much in front of his mother. 'Not *in* the city exactly,' she told him, 'but not far out. We rent a suite of rooms above a couple of shops at St Leonard's, along the Pacific Highway. And, yes, of course I have a business card.'

'Of course,' he murmured, and she shot him a sav-

age glance, which, unfortunately, he couldn't really
see. But she was about to remedy that!

Taking off her sunglasses, she scooped up her handbag from where she'd dropped it beside her chair,
snapped it open and dropped the glasses inside. Then
she opened the side pocket where she kept her business cards and took out three, handing one to Kathryn
and two to Philip.

'Perhaps you could give one to your fiancée,' she
suggested with a sickly-sweet smile. 'Which reminds
me, Kathryn, you said something earlier about the
wedding date only being ten weeks away, and the
bride going to be absent overseas for a lot of that time?
Is that right?'

'Yes, Corinne does voluntary work for one of those
world charities for children. Her best friend is em-
ployed by them as a nurse. Unfortunately, Corinne organised this trip to Indonesia before Philip asked her
to marry him, and she doesn't want to let her friend
down.'

'How very commendable,' Fiona remarked, while
privately thinking it was still an odd time to be going
away. 'Well, if that's the case, then there's no time to
waste, is there? I should meet with the bride very soon
and find out exactly what she wants. It doesn't give
us much time.'

'I'll get Corinne to ring you tonight,' Philip offered.
'On which number? Your mobile?'

'No. I have a firm rule never to use my mobile on
a Sunday unless I have a wedding on. Otherwise I
never have any peace. Here, give me the card back
and I'll jot down my home number.' She extracted a
pen from her bag and added her personal number to
the two already on the card.

'What time would be best for you?' Philip asked after she'd handed the card back to him.

'Any time before eight-thirty.'

'Going out, are you?'

Actually, Fiona rarely went out on a Sunday night. She liked to curl up on front of the telly and watch one of the Sunday night movies which always started at eight-thirty. During the ads she did her nails and got her clothes ready for the working week ahead. Today she'd already done her manicure, and tonight they were re-running one of her all-time favourite films.

The slightly mocking tone in Philip's voice, however, stung her into lying.

'Yes, I am, actually,' she said, and found another of those sweet smiles for him.

'Anywhere special?'

'Not really. Just visiting a friend.'

'Boyfriend?'

'I think Mark's a little old to be called a boyfriend.'

'How old *is* he?' Philip persisted.

'Late thirties.'

'What does he do?'

'Philip, really!' his mother exclaimed, and threw Fiona a look of helpless exasperation. 'See what I mean? Lawyers! They can't help themselves.'

'I'm just making conversation,' Philip said, sounding innocent. But Fiona knew he wasn't doing any such thing. He was deliberately trying to goad her. And he'd succeeded.

But no way was he going to know that.

'It's perfectly all right, Kathryn,' she said nonchalantly. 'I don't mind. Mark's a doctor,' she directed, straight at Philip. 'A surgeon. We met at a dinner party…oh, about six months ago. We've been dating ever since.'

Actually, it had only been three months. It just seemed like six. Mark had all the superficial qualities she found attractive in a man, being tall, dark-haired and good-looking, as well as well-read and intelligent. He was also more than adequate in bed.

But his vanity was beginning to grate and, even worse, he was starting to hint that it was time he settled down and passed on his 'perfect' genes. She'd been going to break with him this week, but now revised that decision. Mark was best kept around till Philip was safely married and out of her life once more.

Fiona felt confident she no longer loved Philip, but there was still an unfortunate chemistry there between them. She could feel it sparking away every time she looked at him. She suspected Philip could feel it too, and resented it as bitterly as she did. That was why he was taking pot-shots at her personal life.

'So where did you meet Corinne?' Fiona asked, deflecting the conversation away from her personal life and back onto Philip's.

'I can't rightly remember. At some charity do she organised, I think.'

'It sounds like she does a lot of charity work.'

'She does.'

Which meant she didn't have a real job. A rich man's daughter, obviously. Well, what had she expected? Philip moved in those kinds of circles.

'How old is she?'

'Twenty-four.'

Just as she'd thought. Young. 'Blonde?'

'Uh-huh.' Again, just as she'd thought. Philip had told her once how much he liked blonde hair.

'Pretty, I've no doubt.'

'Very.'

'She'll make a lovely bride,' Kathryn joined in warmly. 'It's a pity her mother isn't alive to see her. I went to school with her mother, would you believe? But she died when Corinne was a little girl. Corinne's father is George Latham. He's a state senator. You might have heard of him?'

Who hadn't? George Latham was not a shrinking violet, either in size or personality. He was also filthy rich. Or his family was. Yep, Fiona had this wedding tagged correctly. It would be society though and through. Owen would be so pleased.

A sudden beeping had Philip standing up and fishing an extraordinarily small mobile phone out of the back pocket of his jeans. 'Excuse me,' he said, and, flipping it open, placed it to his ear. 'Philip Forsythe,' he said as he walked off to one side.

Both women picked up their coffee cups and began to sip, but Fiona could still hear Philip's side of the conversation quite clearly.

'That's great… No, no, I wouldn't mind at all, actually… All right, Corinne… See you soon, my darling.'

He walked swiftly back to the table, but stayed standing while he snapped the phone shut and slid it back into his pocket.

'That was Corinne,' he said. 'She's feeling a bit better and wants me to come over and babysit. I couldn't really say no, given she's leaving in a week or so. Sorry about lunch, Mother, but you and Fiona will still have a lovely time together, planning the wedding of the year.'

'We certainly will, won't we?' Kathryn agreed, and smiled over at Fiona.

Fiona tried to smile back, but it wasn't easy. She was still reeling with shock over how she'd reacted to Philip calling his fiancée 'my darling.' The warmly said endearment had speared straight to her heart, evoking the memory of when he'd first made love to her and first called *her* his darling—his only darling, his most precious darling.

And now, now he was running off to his new darling, no doubt taking her to bed for the rest of the afternoon in one of those long, leisurely lovemaking sessions which he was so expert at. It had been after one of those romantic afternoons in bed ten years ago that he'd confessed to her that one of the condoms he'd used had broken, and her life had been irrevocably ruined.

Fiona's stomach suddenly clenched down hard, then swirled. A clamminess claimed her and her head began to spin. She wasn't sure if she was going to faint, or be sick. Shakily, she got to her feet, scraping the chair back on the flagstones.

Kathryn's eyes flew upwards, alarmed. 'Are you all right, Fiona? You've gone a terrible colour.'

'I... I...'

She didn't speak another word. She barely had time to blink before a blackness swept over her.

Afterwards, Fiona would wonder over the abruptness of her unconscious state. She'd never fainted before, and had always imagined one sort of drifted into it. But it wasn't like that at all. One minute she was awake, then the next...nothing!

She was totally unaware of Philip scooping her up into his arms to safety, before her head could hit the flagstones, or the look of pain which filled his face as he gathered her close and carried her swiftly into the house. She saw and felt nothing till she came to, lying on a large sofa, Philip's handsome face looming over her.

CHAPTER FOUR

'ARE you all right?' he asked worriedly.

She stared up into his beautiful blue eyes, her first woozy thought being that she was glad he'd taken those rotten sunglasses off. For one mad, delusional moment she wallowed in his concerned expression and the gentle tone of his question.

But then she came back to reality. And rationality.

A frown slowly settled on her forehead as she realised what had happened.

'I *fainted*,' she said disbelievingly.

Philip sat back on his heels and smiled a wry little smile. 'Amazing, isn't it?' he murmured. 'You're human, after all.'

His return to sarcasm sped her recovery, both emotionally and physically. Fancy getting all upset and fainting like that! What a foolish female thing to do! Futile, too.

Angry at herself, she sat up abruptly and swung her feet over the side of the sofa, Philip having to hurriedly get out of her way.

'What on earth do you think you're doing?' he said, scrambling to his feet and glaring down at her. 'You should stay lying down for a while. Mother's ringing her doctor.'

'I'm perfectly all right!' Fiona protested, and to prove it she stood up.

Unfortunately, she wasn't quite all right, and

swayed dangerously. Philip took her by the shoulders and forced her back down into a sitting position.

'For pity's sake, Fiona, do as you're told and just sit!' He plonked down in a nearby armchair and shook his head at her as though she were an idiot. 'You fainted dead at our feet, woman. You can't expect us to ignore that fact. We have to check it out.'

'I'm perfectly all right, I tell you,' she insisted. 'It was a simple faint.'

'You just intimated you've never fainted before.'

'Well, I...I've never skipped breakfast before!' she argued.

'Huh! By the feel of you, you skip breakfast a lot.'

She glared over at him. 'Are you saying I'm too thin?'

He shrugged. 'I'm not getting into an argument over a woman's weight. I'm just saying you could do with a few more pounds.'

'Oh, really? I suppose you preferred me when I was fat!'

'You were never fat. Nicely rounded, maybe, but not fat.'

'Then you were the only one in your family who thought so,' she snapped.

He went to open his mouth, but when his mother came into the room, carrying a glass of water and looking worried, he shut it again. 'The doctor's not at home,' Kathryn said as she hurried over. She handed Fiona the water, then sat next to her on the sofa and peered anxiously into her face. 'You still look pale. Would you like Philip to take you to one of those twenty-four-hour medical centres?'

'Certainly not. I'm perfectly all right,' Fiona repeated, and took a sip of the water. 'I was just confessing to Philip that I forgot to have breakfast. I'll be all right once I eat something.'

'Oh, dear, I wish you'd said something,' Kathryn said. 'I would have brought some food with the coffee instead of waiting for lunch. I'll go and make you a sandwich straight away. Brenda prepared us some lovely ham and salad. Just sit right there, dear, and don't move.'

She bustled off again, rather annoying Fiona with her solicitude. This new warm, caring Kathryn took some getting used to!

'You don't have to look so put out,' Philip said sharply. 'She's only being kind.'

Fiona sighed. 'I know. I know. It's just that…'

'You never thought she was capable of kindness?'

Fiona nodded, and Philip sighed.

'I have to admit she was once on the selfish side. And quite a snob. She'd been very spoiled, by her own father and then by mine. Dad adored her. He was a slave to her wishes. But she's changed quite a bit since you last met. She's been through a lot over the past few years. I suppose you heard about Dad dying? It was in all the papers.'

'Yes,' she admitted.

'It wasn't quite as it said in the papers. Dad didn't die peacefully at all. His fight with cancer was very prolonged, and very painful.'

Fiona's heart turned over. Philip's father had been a fair and decent man. He hadn't deserved a long, lingering death. He'd never judged her, like Kathryn had, or made her feel cheap. It was telling, she thought, that Philip called his mother 'Mother' and his father 'Dad.'

Philip seemed lost in his memories of his father for

a few moments, as she was. But then he cleared his throat. 'I guess the death of a loved one changes a person,' he said abruptly. 'Not that Mother's totally changed. She's still a stickler for manners and appearances, as I'm sure you've noticed.'

'I presume Corinne passed the manners and appearance test,' Fiona said a little tartly.

Philip winced. 'Oh, hell! Corinne! I'd forgotten all about her. I'd better give her a ring, tell her I'll be late.'

'Better still,' Fiona said swiftly, before he could flip open his mobile, 'why don't you just go, Philip? There's nothing more you can do here today.'

He hesitated, his handsome face strangely torn.

Fiona could not imagine over what. Surely he'd want to absent himself from her company as quickly as possible.

'If you're still worried about my fainting,' she said, 'then please don't. Neither my health—nor me—are your responsibility. Not till you sign me up for your wedding, that is. After that, you might like to keep me out of bed.'

His left brow arched slightly and Fiona realised what she'd said. Her eyes met his full on, and whilst her heart was racing madly her face remained superbly composed. No way was she going to let Philip rattle her any more with his sarcasm, spoken or unspoken!

'If you insist,' he said drily. 'I'll get Corinne to ring you this evening, *before* eight-thirty. And I'll drop in to your office tomorrow. Say around noon?'

'*Must* you?' she said painfully. 'I'll trust *you* over the fee if you'll trust *me* over the contract. We can see to the business side of things at some later date.'

'Is there some reason why you don't want me to visit you at your office?'

Fiona groaned silently at Philip's cynical tone and suspicious face. He didn't believe her about Owen. He probably thought she'd slept her way into her partnership at Five-Star Weddings and that she spent every second minute having sex on Owen's desk.

'I can't think of any,' she returned frostily. 'I was just trying to make things easy for you. You must be a very busy man, what with all those successful cases you've defended lately.'

'Not so busy that I can't take some time to make sure my wedding day is a resounding success. I would like to see some of those letters of recommendation you mentioned, along with that portfolio of photographs. Afterwards, if everything is as you say, then I'll take you to lunch and you can run a few ideas by me.'

Inside Fiona, everything fluttered wildly. Outside, she looked perfectly calm. 'Thank you so much,' she said coolly, 'but I don't do business that way.'

'Would Owen object if I took you to lunch?'

'No, but Corinne might.'

He laughed. 'I doubt it. We don't have that kind of relationship.'

'What kind is that?'

'Possessive. Jealous.'

'Really? What kind *do* you have?'

'The kind which will last. The kind which is soundly based on shared goals and things in common rather than some fleeting passion.'

'Sounds pretty boring to me.'

'Not at all. Corinne and I enjoy each other's company a great deal. But we're not compelled to rip each other's clothes off every time we meet.'

Fiona flinched at the reminder of just how passionate *their* relationship had once been. Whenever they'd been alone, they simply hadn't been able to keep their hands off each other. They hadn't been able to get naked quickly enough.

'Not that Corinne and I aren't very happy in bed,' Philip swept on, his blue eyes glittering angrily. 'We are. So there's really no danger in your coming to lunch with me. I promise I won't throw you back over the table and eat you up in a burst of sexual frustration.'

Now Fiona flushed, his snarled words evoking another, far more explicit memory: that of Philip doing exactly what he'd just said. It hadn't been a restaurant table, of course. It had been the richly polished walnut dining table in his father's Double Bay apartment.

She'd never felt anything like it, either before or since.

She stared at him, and her treacherous heart took off. He glared back at her, his eyes hard and narrowed.

'Noon tomorrow,' he ground out. '*Be* there!' And, whirling, he stalked from the room.

Five seconds later, the front door banged. A few seconds further on, the Jag roared into life and took off.

Fiona was sitting there, still stunned, when Kathryn came back into the room. 'Don't tell me Philip left without saying goodbye?' She sounded both puzzled and hurt.

Fiona had no idea why she spoke up to smooth over Philip's rudeness, but she did. 'He...he asked me to say goodbye to you for him. He suddenly remembered Corinne and said he had to dash.'

Kathryn looked appeased. 'Oh…oh, well, I suppose there's not much he could do here, anyway. Men are so useless when it comes to things like weddings. Just tell them what to wear and point them in the direction of the church on the day. That's about all you can do. But we wouldn't be without them, would we?' she added, smiling softly.

'Er…no, I guess not. Thank you,' she added, when Kathryn handed her a plate with a very tasty-looking sandwich on it, cut into dainty little triangles. She picked one up and took a bite, only then realising that her excuse for fainting was probably partially true. She *hadn't* bothered with breakfast. She'd been too obsessed with getting her appearance just right.

'I hope you don't think I'm prying, dear,' Kathryn said a little hesitatingly from where she'd sat down in the armchair Philip had vacated, 'but this fainting business. You…er…couldn't be in the family way, could you?'

Fiona spluttered in shock.

Finally, she gulped the mouthful of sandwich down, and tried to look calmer than she felt. 'No, Kathryn,' she managed. 'No, I'm not. Definitely not.' She'd always made sure nothing like that could ever happen to her again. Never, ever! She was secretly on the pill, as well as insisting any partner she had use protection.

Kathryn nodded. 'That's good, then. I hope you're not offended by my asking, but girls these days have babies all the time without a wedding ring on their finger. You said you had a boyfriend, so I thought…well…'

She smiled apologetically. 'Still, you did say your

friend was a doctor, didn't you? Hopefully, a doctor would know better than to get his girlfriend pregnant.'

'Hopefully,' Fiona said, thinking how Mark was no more to be trusted than any other man when it came to using a condom. She couldn't count the number of times she'd had to remind him.

'The reason pregnancy popped into my mind,' Kathryn went on, 'is because I always fainted in the early weeks of my pregnancies.'

Fiona blinked, then frowned. 'Pregnancies? But I thought…'

'Yes, Philip *is* my only child,' Kathryn admitted. 'But I had several miscarriages before I finally carried full term. My husband and I were warned not to have any more after Philip, so we didn't.

'A pity,' she added softly. 'An only child is never a good idea.'

'Why? Because they get spoiled?'

'Oh, no, Philip was never spoiled,' she denied firmly. 'Not in the slightest. Malcolm brought him up with a very firm hand. Unfortunately, my husband had a tendency to push and pressure the boy too much. Philip had to be the best at everything. School. Sport. Games. Given Philip's equally strong will, it was a recipe for disaster.'

'Disaster?' Fiona echoed weakly.

Kathryn shook her head. 'I don't like to think about that time any more. It's too distressing. Enough to say that when Philip left home to live on campus at university, he rebelled. Amongst other things, he got this most unsuitable girl pregnant, then wanted to drop out of university to marry her.'

'What…what happened?' Fiona choked out, unable to take another bite of the sandwich in her hand.

'She lost the baby. On their wedding day. Afterwards, Malcolm arranged for their marriage to be annulled. Oh, I shouldn't be telling you this, but for some strange reason I feel like I can talk to you. You don't mind, do you?'

All Fiona could do was shake her head.

Kathryn sighed. 'I tell myself everything turned out for the best, especially now that Philip's going to marry Corinne, but sometimes I wonder and worry about that poor girl. I didn't treat her very well, and I regret that now. I hope things turned out all right for her too.'

The room fell awkwardly silent, with Fiona's emotions a mess. She ached to blurt out the truth, that *she* was that poor girl, but what good would such a confession do? Kathryn would be embarrassed, and possibly distressed. Philip would be furious with her. So would Owen.

And she…she would be…what?

Healed?

The idea was laughable. Nothing would heal what had happened to her on that day. It had killed more than her baby. It had killed part of her soul.

But it was still good to hear that Kathryn was sorry for how she'd treated her. Philip was right. She *had* changed.

'It wasn't just the girl I worried about,' Kathryn went on, and Fiona stiffened. 'It was Philip. He wasn't the same afterwards. He lost interest in his studies. He just scraped through his exams that year. He even lost interest in girls. To be honest, I thought he would never fall in love again and marry. Eventually, he did start dating again. No one special, however. Or permanent…

'But then he met Corinne,' she continued, much more cheerily. 'She's just the girl for him. They get along so well. Never a cross word together. She's so sweet. No one could ever be angry with her. Best of all, she wants what *he* wants. A family. Straight away too. That's why their engagement is so short. She doesn't care about a career. She just wants to be Philip's wife and the mother of his children. She simply *adores* children.'

Fiona forced herself to eat the rest of the sandwich, though it was like lead in her stomach.

'I'm sorry, dear,' Kathryn said. 'I really shouldn't be bothering you with this.'

Fiona rallied with an effort. 'No, no, it's all right. I like to get to know the personal side of people whose weddings I work on. I suppose you'll be wanting a big wedding?'

'Oh, yes! I've waited this long to see my son happily married. Nothing's too good for him. Or for Corinne.'

'A church wedding?' Fiona asked, automatically thinking of the small non-denominational church she and Philip had been married in. She'd worn a white suit, despite Kathryn's pointedly hurtful remark about the inappropriateness of the colour.

She hadn't worn white since.

'Actually, no,' Kathryn said. 'Philip insists on a celebrant and Corinne agreed. She said whatever he wanted was okay by her. She's like that. Still, I suppose the garden here would be a nice setting for a wedding, come October,' Kathryn said. 'As long as it doesn't rain.'

'The wedding date's in October?'

'Yes, the last Sunday of the month. Corinne gets back from Indonesia the Friday night of that week.'

'She won't be jet-lagged?'

'She says not. So, as you can see, we don't have that much time.'

'You're right there. Well, first things first. The invitations.' Fiona straightened her shoulders and slipped into her working persona, all brisk efficiency. 'Have you prepared a guest list?'

'Yes. I got Corinne to do that last weekend. I'm afraid it's rather large. Just over two hundred.'

'Don't worry. They won't all come. Has Corinne told you what she wants, or do you have *carte blanche* to make all decisions?'

'I'm to make all the decisions. Corinne says she trusts my taste completely.'

Fiona couldn't make up her mind if this Corinne was clever, lazy, or just not too interested in her own wedding. She'd never known a bride like it. Still, maybe Philip's fiancée was one of those rare creatures: a society girl who wasn't vain, or spoiled, or selfish.

'Naturally, Corinne wants to choose her wedding dress,' Kathryn went on. 'Though she said she's happy to buy off-the-peg. Now you'll have to get her right onto that. She leaves in just over a week, and finding the right dress can sometimes take days.'

'I'll get her right onto that tomorrow, Kathryn. Now don't you worry. That's my job, making sure the families of the bride and groom really enjoy the wedding and don't end up having a nervous breakdown. People think of weddings as a happy time, but, believe me, they can be very stressful for those concerned. Things can get way out of hand.'

'Yes, so I've heard. But I have a feeling my son's

wedding is going to be a wonderful experience with you at the helm, Fiona. Oh, I'm so glad you were recommended. I can already tell you're going to be a godsend, and Philip's wedding is going to be the talk of the town for years to come!'

CHAPTER FIVE

FIONA closed the door of her flat, locked it, turned the air-conditioning up to warm, in deference to the approaching evening, then moved with tired steps down the hallway and into her bedroom. There, she slumped down on the side of the bed, kicked off her shoes, and fell back sideways against the pillows, her feet lifting onto the soft duvet, her eyes closing.

She'd never been so tired in all her life. It was only six o'clock, but it felt as if she'd been up for a week. Mental and emotional exhaustion, she supposed.

She could not move a muscle. She just lay there, mulling over everything that had happened that day.

Nothing, Fiona finally decided, had worked out as she'd thought it would when she'd woken that morning. Except perhaps for Kathryn not recognising her. Now *that* she'd expected!

But the woman herself had certainly come as a surprise. Fiona had found herself responding to Kathryn's new warmth, whether she'd wanted to or not.

Actually, once Philip had left, lunch and the afternoon had gone very well. If she'd been meeting his mother for the first time that day she would have liked her very much indeed. At sixty, Philip's mother had become a surprisingly sweet person, easy to talk to, very reasonable and willing to listen.

If it wasn't for Philip, Fiona would have no problems doing this wedding.

Unfortunately, Philip existed, not just in her memory now, but in reality. Worse, she was still attracted to him, whether she wanted to be or not. Circumstances and time could kill love, Fiona accepted ruefully, but it seemed sexual chemistry was not conducive to reason.

Thank heavens she didn't stir *him* the same way!

Her earlier impression that her own unwanted feelings were mutual couldn't be so, now that she thought about it. Philip had made it perfectly clear she was no longer his type. He didn't like her being a brunette, or thinner. He certainly didn't like her being a career woman. Or having a mind of her own.

Probably that was what had irritated him so much: her being so different from how he remembered.

Fiona thought about Noni for a moment, and the sort of the girl *she'd* been. A lot different from Fiona!

Noni had been curvy and cuddly, with her bottle-blonde hair worn fluffed out and wavy and feminine. She'd dressed in short skirts and tight tops to show off what she'd thought was her simply 'stunning' figure.

She shuddered now to think of it.

But it hadn't just been Noni's physical attributes Philip had been attracted to, Fiona began to see. It had been Noni herself. Naive, dumb, easily impressed Noni, who'd thought her rich, hunky, clever boyfriend was almost god-like. Noni had adored Philip so much she'd have done anything for him.

And she *had* in the end, she thought bitterly.

Fiona was Noni's opposite in every way. Smart, slimmed down and sophisticated, with sleek black hair and a not so amenable manner. She didn't dress to be provocative, or seductive. Her clothes fitted the image she wanted to project: that of a businesswoman, with her *career* at the forefront of her mind, never a man.

Fiona was willing to bet her bottom dollar that Corinne was the sweetly feminine and adoring type, who always deferred to Philip and made him feel ten feet tall. She would be on the voluptuous side, with long blonde hair. During the day she would wear flowing dresses, pink lipsticks and floral perfumes. At night she would display her curves in more glamorous gowns which, whilst not provocative, would still display her hour-glass figure and more than adequate bosom.

Philip had always had a thing for breasts.

The telephone ringing on her bedside table snapped Fiona out of her acid reverie. Frowning, she reached over to pick up the receiver, at the same time casting a quick glance at her watch. Only six-twenty. Could it be Corinne already? Hopefully, it wasn't Mark. Or…God forbid…Philip.

'Fiona Kirby,' she said, in her best business voice.

'So you're home at last!'

Fiona heaved a somewhat relieved sigh. 'Yes, Owen. I'm home.'

'I tried half an hour ago.'

'I just got in.'

'Well, how did it go? I've been dying to know. Couldn't wait till the morning.'

'It went well. I've got the job.'

'What? *You've* got the job! So Mrs Forsythe doesn't mind about…you know?'

'She doesn't mind because she didn't recognise me and she doesn't know.'

Owen's groan sounded tortured.

'Don't panic, Owen. My ex dropped in unexpectedly soon after I arrived, and, yes, he *did* recognise me. But he didn't let on to his mother, so Mum's the word, so to speak. He told me privately not to worry, to take the job and we'll pretend we only just met for the first time today.'

'Really? That was surprisingly nice of him. Still, you *did* say he was nice, didn't you?'

'I did. But, to be truthful, Philip's not quite as nice as he used to be. He's a hot-shot trial lawyer these days, with an attitude to match. Hiring me as his wedding co-ordinator is more a matter of diplomacy and expediency than niceness. For one thing, Mummy dearest was already impressed with the new me, and he didn't want to disappoint her. On top of that, the wedding's only ten weeks off, so they haven't really got much time to shop around. Mrs Forsythe offered double our usual fee, I might add.'

'My God, how did you manage *that*?'

'Accidentally, I can assure you. I was trying to worm my way out of things in the beginning, and said I was very heavily booked at the moment. Mrs Forsythe immediately jumped in with the double fee offer. You know what rich people are like. They think they can buy anything.'

'And they can, the lovely spoiled darlings!' Owen gushed enthusiastically. 'Double our usual fee! Wow, Fiona, that's simply great!'

'Don't count your chickens, Owen. Philip's dropping by the office tomorrow around noon. He wants to see my letters of recommendation and the portfolio of photographs before he puts his John Henry on the contract.'

'That'll be just a formality. No one has better credentials than you.'

'That's what I thought. Oh, and afterwards, he's taking me to lunch.'

'Oh-oh.'

'It's not like that, Owen. Believe me. It's just plain old male curiosity masquerading as politeness.'

'I hope so, dear heart. We don't want any nasty complications, do we? So try not to look too sexy tomorrow.'

'Don't be ridiculous, Owen. I *never* look sexy in my work clothes.'

Owen rolled his eyes. Was the woman blind? Why did she think she had men panting after her all the time? 'Still, I suggest you leave that darling black suit you bought recently at home,' he advised. 'In fact, leave *all* your black clothes at home. Go for grey. Or even brown. Now brown's a passion-killer, if ever there was a colour.'

Fiona laughed. 'You don't have to worry, Owen. It won't matter what I wear. I'm no longer Philip's type.'

'Yeah, but is he still *your* type?'

'Only superficially.'

'That the part I'm worried about.'

'Oh, for pity's sake,' she snapped. 'Do you or do you not want Five-Star Weddings to handle this wedding? Make up your mind!'

'A Forsythe wedding, at double our usual fee? You have to be joking! I'd turn a blind eye to just about anything for that!'

'Then do shut up, Owen, and just hang up. You're tying up the line and I'm expecting the bride to give me a call any moment.'

He hung up.

Fiona sighed irritably and flopped the receiver back

into its cradle, rolling back over and staring up at the ceiling.

'Damn you, Philip,' she muttered, after a minute or two. 'And damn you too, Owen. I'll wear black if I want to!'

Hauling herself off the bed, she scooped up her tan shoes and carried them over to the walk-in robe. There, she placed them neatly in the empty spot on the shoe-rack, then began to undress, carefully hanging up her suit on specially padded hangers. Once down to her undies, she wandered back into the bedroom and into the *en suite* bathroom. There, she stripped off totally, popped her undies and stockings into the basin and turned on the hot tap.

Hand-washing her smalls was a habit she'd got into many years before, when she'd lived in a one-room bedsit which hadn't had a laundry. She still did it that way, despite her present well-appointed apartment having an internal laundry with an excellent washing machine and dryer.

Fiona was down to the rinsing part when she caught a glimpse of her naked body in the vanity mirror, her full breasts jiggling left and right with the washing action. Philip's sneaky remark about her needing a few more pounds popped back into her mind.

He was wrong, she thought tartly. Okay, so she was a good deal lighter than when he'd known her, but she still had a decent bust, a rounded derrière and great legs. Admittedly, her arms were on the slim side, as were her neck and shoulders. Her face no longer had that rounded look, either, but she thought it suited her, with more cheekbones showing and her jawline better defined. Her mouth and eyes looked bigger as well.

Still, maybe Philip *liked* fat women. Owen did.

Maybe Corinne was fat. Or at least pleasantly plump.

No, she couldn't be. Kathryn had said she would make a lovely bride, and Kathryn definitely belonged to the *you can never be too rich or too thin* line of thinking.

No, Corinne wasn't going to be fat. Just shapely. And pretty. Very, very pretty.

The telephone rang again, catching Fiona with her hands still in the sink. Quickly drying them, she hurried, still naked, back into the bedroom, and snatched up the receiver.

'Fiona Kirby,' she answered briskly.

'It's Philip, Ms Kirby. Philip Forsythe.'

Fiona stiffened at both his relaxed drawl and at his deliberate use of both their surnames. Clearly darling Corinne was within listening distance.

Fiona immediately pictured them in bed, as naked as she was, limbs twined, their bodies still warm and sated from their lovemaking.

'Yes, Mr Forsythe?' she drawled back, but there was a brick of ice in her chest.

'Corinne wanted me to make the initial contact for her. She felt a little shy about it. Here she is now...'

Fiona could see him handing his fiancée the receiver, the cord stretching across his bare chest to reach her. His ear would still be so close that he would hear what she had to say.

'Hello? Fiona? This is Corinne.' A pleasant voice. Soft. Lilting. Sweet.

Fiona plastered a smile on her face so that she sounded happy. 'Hi, there, Corinne. Kathryn's been telling me such nice things about you.'

'Has she? How kind of her. Oh, but then, she *is* a darling, isn't she?'

'She certainly is. Now, since time is of the essence, Corinne, I think we should get together as soon as possible. I can't really make a proper plan for the wedding ceremony and reception afterwards till I know what kind of dress you'll be wearing, not to mention the colour you've chosen for the bridesmaids. Everything pivots around that.'

'Oh. Well, actually, I'm not sure what kind of wedding dress I want to wear yet. Carmel's promised to come with me when I choose. She always knows what looks best on me. Carmel's my very best friend. We do simply everything together. But I *can* tell you that there's only going to be the one bridesmaid. That'll be Carmel, of course. And she's decided to wear black.'

'Only *one* bridesmaid?' Fiona repeated, startled. The black bit didn't bother her. Bridesmaids wearing black had come into vogue over the last few years.

'Yes, that's right. Carmel's my only close girlfriend and I don't have any sisters. Neither does Philip, so it seems silly to have a big wedding party just for the sake of it.'

'I see. Well, of course you're the bride, Corinne. I'm here to do whatever you want. It's just that Kathryn implied it would be a big wedding.'

'Oh, it will be, guest-wise. Daddy's inviting all his political cronies. And the Forsythe family seems to just go on and on for ever! Oh, Philip, stop that,' she giggled. 'You know it's true. Those cousins of yours have a baby every week or so. Sorry about that, Fiona. Philip's making faces at me.'

'Really?' Fiona gritted her teeth. 'So! When would

be a convenient time for both you and Carmel to come dress-shopping this week?'

'Any day this week, really. Carmel's on holiday and staying at my place. What's that, Philip? Oh, Philip says not tomorrow, of course. *He's* coming to see you tomorrow. What, Philip?'

Fiona hung on grimly while a male voice muttered in the background. At least they weren't in bed together. Philip sounded too far away for that.

'Philip says he's going to take you out to lunch as a thank-you for dropping everything and doing our wedding. Tell you what, Fiona. Get him to take you to Moby Dick's. It's a new place down at the water-front at The Rocks. Simply scrummy food. You'll like it.'

Fiona grimaced. Darn, but the girl *was* sweet. And with not a jealous bone in her body.

If Philip was *my* fiancé, Fiona thought savagely, I wouldn't let him within cooee of another woman, let alone some unknown female who could be anybody.

Which I am.

'Unfortunately, I simply won't have time for a long lunch, Corinne. It'll have to be a quick coffee down at the local café. So, how about Tuesday? I'll pick you and Carmel up at your place around ten?'

'That'd be great.' And she gave Fiona an address in Mosman.

'Is that where you are now?' some masochistic devil made her ask.

A light, tinkling laugh. 'Oh, no. I'm staying with Philip at his family's Double Bay apartment for the weekend.'

'Ahh. I see…' Which she did.

Fiona closed her eyes and could have wept.

It was wickedly unfair. How *could* she be this jealous over a man she no longer loved?

In desperation, she searched her heart and found a less threatening reason for her intense reactions today.

It's not really jealousy you're feeling, she decided, but envy. You envy Philip's getting over what happened ten years ago. You envy his being able to want normal things, like a wife and a family. You envy his finding someone really nice to share his life with.

And he *has* found someone nice. Clearly Corinne *was* a sweetie. Fiona wanted to hate her, but it was herself she hated, for being so screwed up.

'Philip wants to talk to you again, Fiona,' Corinne suddenly piped up, and Fiona's heart squeezed tight again. 'Here he is. I'm off to make some coffee. See you Tuesday, Fiona.'

'Looking forward to it, Corinne.'

Fiona held her breath till Philip came on the line.

'I may be a little later than noon,' he said straight away, in a businesslike voice. 'I have to be in court first thing in the morning. I shouldn't be held up, but things don't always run smoothly there. So if I'm a bit late, don't worry.'

'Fine,' she returned crisply. 'But, as I was just saying to Corinne, no lunch, thanks. I'm very busy at the moment, as I told you earlier. I haven't time to waste sitting round waiting to be served. I eat on the run most days.'

'When you eat at all, that is,' he drawled.

'What *is* this obsession with my weight?' she snapped. 'I'll have you know I'm the perfect weight for my height. Whether you believe me or not, I used to be *over*weight. If you could see me right at this moment, you would see for yourself than I'm perfectly healthy.'

'Meaning?'

'Meaning I'm standing here in my birthday suit and I have more than enough flesh on my bones to satisfy most men.'

'I'm sure you do, Fiona,' he mocked. 'I'm sure you do. But I'm not most men, and I'm really not interested in your body anymore. All I want from you, sweetheart, is closure.'

'Closure!' What on earth was he talking about?

'That's right. I know it's one of those irritating New Age words, but it rather covers our situation well. There's a couple of questions that I've always wanted to ask you, and a couple more that have arisen since speaking to you today. I want to hear the answers to those questions right from the horse's mouth, so to speak. So I suggest you *make* time for lunch with me tomorrow, madam. Otherwise, Five-Star Weddings won't be getting the lucrative commission for my wedding to Corinne, or the considerable kudos and publicity which will inevitably go with it. Do you get my drift?'

Fiona said nothing. She was furious, yet at the same time flustered. What questions?

'So glad you've finally seen some sense and stopped arguing,' he grated out. 'Just make sure you don't go giving me any trouble tomorrow. About lunch, that is. Oh, and make sure you come prepared to tell the truth, the whole truth and nothing but the truth.'

And he hung up.

CHAPTER SIX

OWEN was standing talking to Janey at Reception when Fiona walked in the next morning. He took one horrified look at her, grabbed her nearest arm and pulled her aside.

'You're wearing black!' he whispered. 'I thought I told you not to wear black!'

Not just any old black, either, Owen groaned silently. But that brand-new black suit of hers, with the tighter than usual skirt, and the nipped-in-at-the-waist jacket which made her bottom look bigger and gave even Owen lewd ideas. When combined with the black satin cami underneath, shiny black hose and those lethal stiletto heels, she looked all respectability on top, but with the promise of smoulder underneath.

One of Fiona's darkly winged brows lifted, and she eyed him with that don't-cross-me-or-you'll-be-sorry look. It had extra impact that morning, perhaps because she was wearing more eye make-up than usual. And more lipstick. *And* more perfume, he noted worriedly.

Her lack of jewellery wasn't a plus because its absence seemed to emphasise her striking dark beauty. Owen stared at the sleek curtain of black hair which was hooked somewhat carelessly behind an ear on one side, then at the long pale column of her throat, bare of all adornment. He thought she'd never looked more seductive.

'I'll wear whatever colour I like,' she said frostily.

'And whatever I like. Please don't go jumping to false and quite stupid conclusions here, Owen. I haven't dressed this way for Philip Forsythe. Mark is picking me up after work tonight. We're going out to dinner.'

Owen frowned. 'But I thought you said you were going to give Mark the heave-ho.'

Her smile was wry. 'I really should stop gossiping to you over my morning coffee. Still, it's a woman's privilege to change her mind, isn't it? I *am* still a woman,' she added waspishly, 'despite some people seeming to think I'm a cross between a robot and a scarecrow.

'Janey,' she rapped out, whirling to face the startled receptionist. 'Send Rebecca straight into me as soon as she arrives. Oh, and there will be a Mr Forsythe dropping by to see me around noon. When he arrives, please let me know he's here, but have him wait till I come and get him. Okay?'

Eyes like iced chocolate swung back to Owen. 'I'm afraid I won't have time for a morning tea-break this morning, Owen. I have too much work to do. My partner *will* insist on signing me up for more work than any normal human being can handle. There again, I'm not human, am I? I'm a machine!'

Owen watched her stalk off down the corridor, the premonition of doom dampening yesterday's optimism over getting the Forsythe wedding. All he could do was try to prevent anything dreadful happening, and protect the business come what may.

'Janey,' he whispered. 'Don't let Fiona know when Mr Forsythe arrives. Show him into my office first. I'll take him along to Fiona after a few minutes.'

'Okey dokey, boss,' Janey said, and smiled a conspiratorial smile.

She did just that, and shortly before noon Philip Forsythe was ushered quietly into Owen's office.

The sight of the groom instantly increased Owen's worries. The man was everything Fiona went for, only more so. Better built. Better-looking. And a better dresser.

Still, so he should be, Owen thought ruefully, with all that Forsythe money behind him.

Owen was an expert in clothing of all kinds, and he knew exactly what that sleek navy suit had cost. Combine it with the blue handmade silk shirt, designer printed tie and exclusive Italian shoes, and you had an outfit the price of which would have fed a family of four for a year.

Owen rose from behind his desk and stretched a hand across in welcome. The hand that shook his in return was firm, and strong, and unwavering. Owen hoped his love for his fiancée was just as firm and strong and unwavering.

'How do you, Mr Forsythe?' he greeted him. 'I'm Owen Simpson, Fiona's partner in Five-Star Weddings. I'll take you along to Fiona in a minute. I'd just like to have a few words before I do, if you don't mind. Do please sit down.'

A couple of minutes passed in idle chit-chat, during which they exchanged banal pleasantries and got down to first names before Owen brought up what was bothering him.

'I have to admit to some concern with this hiding of Fiona's true identity, Philip. What will happen if your mother suddenly recognises her wedding co-ordinator as her long-lost daughter-in-law?'

'Believe me,' the groom said very drily, 'that won't happen.'

'How can you be so sure? Is Fiona so very different these days?'

The corner of his client's mouth lifted into a small sardonic smile. 'As different as two people can get.'

'But *you* recognised her.'

Owen was stunned by the stark emotion which flitted across the far too handsome face. Admittedly, the flash of pain was only momentary, but it was strong, and deep.

'Ahh, yes...I recognised her,' he admitted on a raw note. 'Instantly.'

Alarm bells started ringing in Owen's brain. If ever he'd heard the sounds of a tortured soul, it had been then. Whatever had happened ten years ago, to end Philip's marriage to Fiona, it had not been due to lack of emotional involvement on this man's part. It worried Owen that Philip's one-time love for his ex-wife might be too easily revived.

Fiona's assertion that she was no longer Philip's physical type could very well be true, but he wasn't willing to risk it.

On top of that, he felt it was his male duty to warn Philip exactly what sort of girl Fiona was these days when it came to men. Owen had an old-fashioned attitude to marriage, and a strong aversion to infidelity of any kind.

Admittedly, Fiona had never tangled with a married man's affections before—or an engaged one, for that matter—but even he could see this was an unusual situation. They'd been married before, for pity's sake, already been to bed together. Fiona would know exactly what this man liked when it came to matters of the boudoir.

'You know, Philip, I was quite shocked to learn the

other day that Fiona had been married,' he piped up. 'Not once, but twice! Did you…er…know about her second marriage?'

'I did, actually,' came the taut reply.

Oh, yes, he still felt something for Fiona. Owen was sure of it. And she still felt something for him, the wicked little minx. She hadn't tarted herself up today for some dinner with Mark. Mark was on the way out. Owen knew the signs.

'Well, Fiona's certainly not the marrying kind of girl these days,' Owen said, with a knowing little laugh. 'In the six years I've known her, that girl's had more men-friends than Henry the Eighth had wives. She tires of them just as quickly too. Still…maybe she's always been like that, eh, what? Maybe after two divorces she finally learned not to promise to love, honour and cherish till death do us part—because she knew what she really meant was till six months us do part.'

Forsythe didn't say a word, but his expression was hard, his blue eyes cold.

'I doubt she'll ever marry again,' Owen added. 'She doesn't want children for starters. Not much point in marriage without children, is there?'

'Not much,' the ex bit out.

'And it's not as though a girl has to marry to have a sex-life these days. Certainly not girls who look like Fiona. She has men panting after her all the time. Pity most of them are stupid enough to fall in love with her, though. There's no future in falling in love with career girls like Fiona. They have only one use for men and it isn't to marry them.'

There was a short, sharp silence, during which Philip Forsythe just sat there, stony-faced.

Satisfied that he'd got his message across, Owen jumped to his feet. 'I'd better take you along to Fiona's office before she wonders where you are. But for pity's sake, don't tell her what I just said. She's very touchy about her private life.'

'Don't worry. I won't breathe a word. What Fiona does in her private life these days is not of the slightest interest to me.'

Despite the cold disdain in Philip's voice, Owen was not totally convinced. He'd much rather have heard indifference.

Still, he'd done his best. What more could he do?

CHAPTER SEVEN

AT FIVE minutes to twelve, Fiona sent Rebecca back to her own office, nerves finally getting the better of her.

She'd come to work this morning, fired up with resentment over Philip's high-handed attitude on the telephone. Who did he think he was, treating her like some hostile witness on the stand? No way was she going to let him grill her about the past. She'd spent ten years getting over what had happened back then and she wasn't about to relive it. Neither was she going to reexplain her actions and decisions.

She'd been steady as a rock in her resolve till around eleven, when the reality of a long lunch alone with Philip had begun to unnerve her. By eleven-thirty she'd started clock-watching and waiting for the phone to ring, announcing his arrival.

For the last twenty-five minutes, however, her phone had remained stubbornly silent, a perverse state of affairs when, on most Monday mornings, she had little peace from its infernal and eternal ringing.

Fiona glared at the darned thing, but it just sat there, mutely mocking her growing agitation. She was reminded of a scene from one of those movies where the condemned man is be executed at midnight and the camera keeps going to the clock on the wall, then to the telephone just below it. Tension builds as the audience hopes and prays for the powers that be to call with a stay of execution.

77

That rarely happened, and the poor fellow was duly led away.

Fiona could not imagine anything worse than knowing the exact time of one's death. The mental agony for the executee would be excruciating.

Fiona's own tension was excruciating by the time the hands on the wall-clock finally came together at noon. Yet the phone—and her office—stayed deathly silent, the double glazed windows blocking out the noise of the traffic below, the solid walls and door stopping any sounds filtering through from the adjoining rooms.

Normally, Fiona liked this aspect of the solid old building. Today she found the silence claustrophobic.

By five past twelve she felt as if she was about to burst!

Jumping to her feet, she began to pace agitatedly around the room, muttering to herself.

When the phone suddenly jangled, her stomach leapt through her chest and into her mouth. For a few seconds she froze, before launching herself back to her desk and snatching up the receiver.

'Yes?' she asked rather breathlessly.

It wasn't Janey, announcing Philip's arrival. It was one of the florists she used, wanting to check up on a few things for the following weekend's wedding.

More frustration flared, and Fiona had to fight for composure. Scooping in a deep breath, she slid up onto the corner of her somewhat battered but large desk, firmly crossed her legs, and found a cool voice from somewhere.

Experience had taught her that if she sounded and acted as though she were totally in control, soon she was. Fiona was actually idly swinging her top foot and answering the florist's questions quite calmly when there was a soft tap on her office door. Before she had time to do more than blink, the door opened and Owen popped his head inside.

'Excuse me for a sec,' she told the florist. 'What is it, Owen?'

'Er...you were on the phone, so Janey brought Philip along to me for a minute. Is it all right for him to come in now?'

An instant vice clamped around Fiona's chest, whilst a thousand fluttering butterflies invaded her stomach.

Now you just stop this, she hissed to herself. He's just a man, not some dark and dangerous nemesis. Get a grip!

'Fine,' she told Owen with seemingly blithe indifference. 'I'll just be a moment or two longer. Have him come in and sit down.'

She swung her body slightly away from the doorway so that she wasn't facing Philip when he entered the room. That way she wouldn't have to look straight at him, or smile, or do anything except pretend to be thoroughly engrossed in a discussion over what blue flowers could be substituted if forget-me-knots were still unavailable this week. Out of the corner of her eye, however, she glimpsed him coming in alone, shutting the door behind him and settling his tall, elegantly clad frame into the comfy sofa which rested against the wall not far from the door.

'So long as they're blue and not mauve, Gillian,' she was saying coolly, despite being hotly aware of Philip's gaze on her legs, and the expanse of thigh her perched position was displaying.

Still, she would look ridiculous if she hastily uncrossed her legs, yanked down her skirt and pressed her knees firmly together like some uptight virgin.

Philip had seen a lot more of her bare than her thighs, anyway.

The thought made her insides tense. Was he sitting there, looking at her legs and remembering?

Fiona had been overawed and shy with him at first, but not for long. After their first stunning time together, she'd eagerly let him remove all her clothes, plus every one of her other remaining inhibitions and misconceptions about making love.

Though not a physical virgin when they'd met, she'd been a virgin in every other way, totally ignorant of the mindless madness which overtook a girl when deeply in love, and utterly unprepared for the bittersweet pleasures of the flesh just waiting to enslave her.

And enslave her Philip had. With breathtaking speed and an equally breathtaking expertise. By the time they'd been going out for a month, she'd been beside herself with desire for him, blown away by an unquenchable passion which had known no taboos. She'd done everything he'd wanted, sometimes before he'd asked. She'd been his besotted love-slave, his never-say-no Noni.

Once had never been enough…for either of them.

Fiona gritted her teeth at the memory and chatted on about the flowers, feigning indifference to Philip's presence, idly swinging her foot again.

But, for all her outer nonchalance, behind her constricted ribs her heart had begun racing madly. A faint flush was wending its wicked way over the surface of her skin, bringing a prickling sensation to the erogenous zones of her body. Her breasts felt swollen, a disconcerting state of affairs since they weren't safely encased in a bra. Her nipples peaked like hot pokers against the cool black satin of her camisole. Her neck felt decidedly warm, as did her face.

The temptation to pick up a nearby writing pad and fan herself was acute. All her clothes suddenly felt far too hot and far, far too tight.

Instead, with her free hand, she reached down and popped open the waist button on her jacket, sucking in some much needed air between words. 'Yes…yes… That would be fine… Now I must go… A client… Yes, no rest for the wicked.' She gave a soft if somewhat shaky laugh. 'Bye, Gillian.'

She hung up, and without looking at Philip slipped off the corner of the desk, firmly rebuttoning her jacket as she strode round behind her desk. Only when she was safely seated in her chair did she glance up at him.

Just as well too, for he *was* staring at her. He was also looking sinfully sexy in one of those dark single-breasted suits which she simply adored on a man.

Not that Philip needed clothes to make him attractive to her. To her eye, he looked fantastic in anything. He looked extra fantastic in nothing.

Fiona gulped at this thought, having to battle to keep her mind back off *that* track. It had been bad enough imagining he was mentally undressing *her* whilst she'd been sitting on her desk. If she started stripping *him* in her mind, she would soon be *non compos mentis*.

But it was difficult *not* to look at him and wonder what he looked like now naked. He had more muscle on him now, more breadth of shoulder and overall solidity. Fiona didn't doubt that the more mature

Philip would be even more impressive in the buff than he had been at twenty.

And that was saying something.

Because he'd been pretty impressive back then.

Fiona had never seen the like, either before or since.

It was not a good thought to have in her head whilst trying to stay cool, calm and collected.

Clearing her throat, she looked down at her desk and turned some papers and a folder round to face his way.

'I have all the things ready you asked to look at,' she began brusquely. 'The letters of recommendation. The portfolio of photographs. Plus a sample contract for you to peruse at your leisure.

'If you'd like to come a little closer…' she added, glancing up again at long last.

Their eyes met. His were hard and cold. Hers were hopefully businesslike and pragmatic.

Rising abruptly, his hand reached for the nearby doorknob. 'That can wait till later,' he said curtly as he yanked open the door. 'I'm in a fifteen-minute parking spot, and my time is about to run out.'

Her mouth opened automatically to argue, but she immediately thought better of it. To argue with him was to betray emotion. Fiona didn't want Philip to know that he still had the power to affect her in any way whatsoever.

Rising, she grabbed her black handbag, hoisted the long strap over her shoulder, then, with one hand firmly on its top flap and the other swinging by her side, covered the expanse of patterned carpet between her desk and the door with confident strides.

'Where are we going?' she asked nonchalantly as she brushed past him.

His answer floored her.

'Balmoral Beach.'

She swung round and almost collided with him, momentarily putting her hand on his chest to steady herself, but swiftly snatching it away as though she'd stupidly reached out to stroke a cobra.

'If you think I'm going to go with you to your place,' she hissed, from still far too close a position, 'then you can think again!'

His eyes showed surprise at her reaction, then a measure of thoughtfulness. 'How do you know I live at Balmoral?'

Fiona thanked the Lord she could think on her feet. 'Your mother told me.'

'*Did* she?'

'Yes, she did. Why?' she challenged. Aggression was always the best defence when you were caught at a disadvantage.

He shrugged his beautifully tailored shoulders. 'I just wondered how you knew. But there's no reason to panic. I'm not taking you to my place. I've made a booking at the Watermark restaurant for lunch. It's right on Balmoral Beach.'

Fiona could not believe the irony of the situation. The Watermark was the very restaurant Mark was planning to take her to that evening after work. He'd raved over how special it was. How exclusive and expensive, with a view second to none and a clientele to match. Meaning he wanted to impress her. Maybe he'd seen the writing on the wall.

'Yes, I know of it,' she said tautly.

Philip smiled a small smile. 'I imagine you would.'

'Meaning?' she snapped.

'Meaning I presume a popular girl like you would have been there before,' he said drily.

'Who says I'm popular?'

His gaze narrowed and swept down over her tensely held body, glaring at where her breasts were throbbing beneath the confines of her jacket.

'Come now, Fiona,' he drawled. 'Much as I might prefer the old version, I'm not blind to your present-day attractions. I would imagine you're never short of a dinner date, or some eager lover, ready and willing to satisfy your no doubt still insatiable needs. His name might be Mark at the moment. But last year it was probably Roger. And next year it could be Tom, Dick, or Harry. The names don't really matter to you, do they? As long as their performance is up to scratch and they don't do the unforgivable thing of hanging around too long and wearing out their welcome.'

Fiona was momentarily stunned by his verbal attack. Fair enough that he might think her a flighty piece, incapable of any depth of feeling or love. She accepted that his low opinion of her loyalty level was the legacy of her lies ten years ago, plus that other unfortunate marriage she'd raced into.

But that didn't call for his virtually calling her a slut!

She wanted to come to her own defence, but stopped herself just in time. Why try to change his opinion of her? There was a certain safety in his misguided judgement of her present-day lifestyle.

'So what?' she flung at him offhandedly. 'What's it to you?'

'Nothing at all,' he returned coldly. 'But I pity your poor Mark.'

She laughed. 'Really? I doubt he needs it, but I'll

pass on your sentiments to him tonight. He's picking me up after work. That's why I'm all dressed up.'

'I never imagined it was for my benefit.'

'How clever of you. Now, shall we get going? You don't want to end up with a parking ticket, do you?'

CHAPTER EIGHT

THE suburb of Balmoral was only a ten-minute drive from where Fiona's office was located at St Leonard's, maybe fifteen if the local council was digging up the Pacific Highway and adjoining roads, which always seemed the case when Fiona was desperate to get somewhere quickly. She'd learnt to allow extra time, on wedding days especially.

But no workmen flagged them down during the brief journey, which was just as well. Being enclosed within a sexy black car which smelt of new leather and Philip's sexy aftershave did nothing for Fiona's state of mind. And body.

Even so, those ten minutes *seemed* like an eternity, despite Fiona taking up where she'd left off back at the office and chattering away as if she hadn't a care in the world. Not easy when, inside, she was wound up tight as a drum.

Philip made no pretence over his own mood, politeness not on his agenda, it seemed. He sat stiffly behind the wheel, his eyes fixed straight ahead, his only contribution to the conversation being one-word replies. By the time they turned down Military Road, and Balmoral was just a sea breeze away, his shoulders did loosen a little, and he stopped gripping the wheel with white-knuckled intensity. His face, however, remained without humour.

Frankly, Fiona could not understand why Philip was still so angry with her. The thought that he'd been pining for her all these years, that *she* might have been the one true love in *his* life, was far too fanciful a theory—and just too awful to contemplate—so she searched for another, more sensible, logical reason.

It dawned on her pretty quickly.

Male ego. Seriously dented at the time, and obviously still bruised.

Yes, that was the most likely cause for the sarcasm yesterday and today. Philip had always had a healthy ego. How could he not with all those God-given talents? Even at the tender age of twenty he would have already been prey to more female pursuits—and willing surrenders—than Fiona could possibly imagine. He hadn't achieved that level of skill as a lover through correspondence!

Fiona had no doubt not a single girlfriend of his had ever voluntarily broken up with him.

Till she'd come along.

Philip probably hadn't experienced rejection before and simply hadn't been able to handle it.

Most men couldn't, Fiona supposed, especially from someone like Noni. Good Lord, even *she* could excuse Philip for believing Noni would be his love-slave for life, the naive, gullible little fool!

But Noni was long gone now, she reaffirmed to herself. Fiona lived and breathed in her place, and Fiona was not naive, or gullible. She certainly wasn't about to put up with being grilled by Philip over the whys and wherefores of their break-up. Heavens, she wouldn't even *dream* of telling him the truth, the whole truth and nothing but the truth.

Masochism was not her thing at all!

She was reminding herself of this fact when the Jaguar smoothly negotiated a downhill corner, and, right before her eyes, the beach suddenly came into view.

Oddly enough, although she'd driven through Balmoral and shopped in its main street, Fiona had never been down to the actual beach before.

Its beauty quite took her breath away.

'Oh,' she gasped softly. 'Oh, how lovely.'

'Yes, it is,' Philip agreed, then slanted her a puzzled look. 'I thought you said you'd been to the Watermark before?'

'No, not actually. I've only heard of it.'

Philip stopped the car at the bottom of the hill and turned right, to drive slowly along the esplanade which hugged the cove-like beach. Fiona drank in the scene, and thought how wonderful it would be to live here and be able to walk down to this place at any time and sit on the warm golden sand, or under the shade of one of the huge trees which lined the pavement.

The water was so blue, and gentle. Not a roaring surf, just lapping waves. Relaxing. Refreshing.

An old-fashioned fenced-off pool stretched out into the bay and there wasn't a single commercial marina in sight, thank heavens, just a few boats, bobbing up and down at their private moorings.

Fiona glanced back up at the houses which hugged the hills overlooking the beach, and envied their own-ers—not so much for the houses themselves, although some of them were very grand, but for the sea view, and the position. They were close to the city yet at the same time a world away, hiding in this perfect oasis of peace and perfection.

It took a few moments before Fiona recalled Philip owned one of those houses.

'You're very lucky to live here,' she said as he directed the Jag into a parking spot facing the beach, plus the biggest Morton Bay fig tree Fiona had ever seen.

'It's not quite so ideal in the summer,' Philip returned drily, turning off the engine and pulling out his keys. 'Wall-to-wall cars, plus wall-to-wall people, all wanting their piece of paradise. But, yes, I have to agree with you. The first time I saw this place I planned to buy a house here, overlooking the ocean. But it took me quite a while to save up the money to buy the sort of house I wanted. I finally managed it last year.'

Fiona frowned over at him. 'I would have thought you could have afforded to buy any house you wanted straight away, being your father's only son and heir.'

'True. But it's a funny thing about inherited money. You don't get nearly as much pleasure and satisfaction spending it as you do the money you've earned yourself.'

'Is that the reason you went into criminal law, instead of corporate law? Because it paid more?'

'Not at all. No, I went into criminal law because corporate manoeuvrings, no matter how conniving or clever, just didn't cut it with my competitive spirit. I never *was* a team player, even when I was a boy at school. I like single-handed combat. Tennis. Judo. Fencing. They were my chosen sports. I never was one for cricket or football.

'Or boardrooms,' he added, and shot her a wry smile. 'The courtroom, however, is much more my style. A gladiatorial arena where man is pitted against man. Blood is let there, believe me. I find it an exciting challenge ensuring that the blood is not mine, or my clients'.'

The passion in his voice sent her heart doing flip-flops inside her chest. That was what separated Philip from the rest of the men she'd known in the past ten years. The intensity of his passion.

'You really love it, don't you?' she murmured.

'I suppose I do,' he said, sounding almost surprised at this self-discovery. 'But why did you say it like that?' And he fixed his intelligent blue eyes on hers. 'Don't you love *your* job?'

Fiona looked away and tried to think.

Did she? There was a certain satisfaction after a wedding of a job well done. But, in truth, it wasn't easy seeing couples so much in love all the time, radiant with joy on their special day, then going off on their honeymoons, full of optimism and happiness. It was a constant reminder of what she'd missed out on, and what she would never have.

'I like being my own boss,' she hedged. 'And it pays well.'

'Money's not everything.'

'Yes, I do know that, Philip,' she defended coolly. 'I'm not as superficial as you seem determined to believe. Even if I was, I'm at a loss to know why the way I live my life nowadays bothers you so much, or even at all!'

His eyebrows lifted and his eyes glittered beneath them. 'It shouldn't, should it?'

'No,' she said firmly.

He actually gave her remark some thought, then pursed his lips before turning cold blue eyes her way. 'You're quite right,' he said curtly. 'You have every right to live your life as you see fit and I have no right to pass judgement on it. If I've been rude, then please accept my apology. It's just that—'

He broke off as something troubling flashed across his eyes, momentarily upsetting his icy equilibrium.

'Just what?' she probed softly, and the muscles in his face stiffened.

'Nothing,' he ground out. 'I can see now that I romanticised our relationship in my memory. Maybe I even romanticised Noni. Maybe she wasn't what I thought. Ever! At the time, I found it hard to believe Noni when she said she'd only married me because of the baby, and that once the baby was gone there was no point in continuing with our marriage. I found it even harder to believe her when she claimed she wasn't really in love with me, that it was just a sexual thing, and that sooner or later it would fizzle out.'

Fiona just stared at him, afraid of where this was leading, fearful that she might have to repeat those old lies all over again.

He laughed. 'No need to look so worried, Fiona, my rose-coloured glasses have fallen away well and truly now. I finally appreciate that you *weren't* lying back then. Sex *was* the only basis of our relationship. Marriage between us would have eventually ended in divorce, as your second marriage did. *I* was the romantic fool. *You* were the sensible one. Yet at the time I could have sworn it was the other way around.'

Fiona's eyes were wide and unwavering upon him.

'In hindsight,' he raved on, 'the truth is now perfectly obvious. I'm surprised I didn't realise it before today. Hell, when did we ever do anything together except make love? We never went out. We never even talked much. We just tore each other's clothes off and did it all the time. That's not love, as you said. It's just sex.'

Fiona flinched at this harsh dismissal of what she'd

always believed the great love of her love. His cold certainty actually raised questions in her own mind. *Had* it just been sex, even on her part? Had she broken her heart over an illusion, one which would have died a natural death if she'd stuck around? Had she made the ultimate sacrifice for nothing?

Her bewildered gaze raked over Philip as she sought for answers.

There were none to be found in looking at him, only more confusion as she began to respond to his beautiful male body on that superficial sexual level which he'd just reminded her of with such perverse honesty. All that talk of how much they'd once made love didn't exactly help. She started thinking of the many times they'd made love in his car back in the old days; how steering wheels and gearsticks had been just minor hurdles to be laughingly got around, with the back seat the ultimate in decadence if they'd thought they could last long enough to climb into the back. They'd invented positions and mutual activities in that small car which the *Kama Sutra* hadn't thought of.

Her breathing grew shallow at the memories, her mouth drying, her head growing light.

A child suddenly ran past the car, laughing loudly. The sound snapped Fiona back to the reality of what was happening to her, both in her mind and body.

Action was called for. Swiftly distracting action! She dredged up her most dazzling and superficial smile, startling a grim-faced Philip with it while she reached for the doorknob.

'So glad we finally got that all sorted out!' she pronounced. 'Now we can go have lunch and sort out something far more important. Your wedding!' And she was out of the car in a flash, pulling her skirt down as far as it would go and breathing in deeply several times.

Philip was slower to alight from his side, and when he did he looked disgruntled.

'I thought we'd decided to leave all the wedding details up to you and my mother,' he said.

'In the main. But I still want to know what *you'd* like.'

'What I'd like, Fiona,' he returned sharply, 'is to simply have lunch without any talk of the wedding at all. Do you think we might leave all that till later, back at your office?'

She felt slightly perplexed by this request. And troubled. His wedding was such a *safe* subject. But she shrugged her acquiescence, determined to keep up the indifferent role she'd chosen to play with him. 'If that's what you want.'

'That's what I want,' he said firmly, and, taking her elbow, began to steer her along the pavement towards a nearby building which she presumed was the Watermark restaurant.

It was.

'Besides,' he added as he stopped abruptly at the door, 'I haven't quite sorted out what happened ten years ago to my total satisfaction. I still have one question to ask you.'

Fiona tried not to look concerned. 'Fine,' she said blithely. 'Ask away.'

'Not right now,' he returned. 'It can wait.' And he let go her arm to pull open the door, and gallantly wave her inside first.

Fiona found a smile from somewhere, and walked past him into the restaurant.

CHAPTER NINE

EVERYONE in the restaurant knew him by name. They were also given one of the best tables in the house, down in a private corner with a view to die for.

Not that the other tables didn't have lovely views. The Watermark wasn't called the Watermark for nothing. It took advantage of its position right on the beach, with huge windows facing the water and a simple, uncluttered decor which didn't distract its patrons from the beauty beyond the glass.

Fiona liked it on sight. And might have said so if she hadn't felt so distracted already. What other question could Philip possibly want to ask her, if he now accepted the things Noni had told him ten years ago? She couldn't begin to imagine what was still bothering him!

On top of that worry, she was still rattled by the questions Philip had raised in her own mind.

Had she loved him or hadn't she?

There was no doubt that her feelings *had* been superficial and strictly sexual out there in the car just now. But that was logical because she definitely no longer loved him.

That didn't mean her feelings for Philip had always been like that. Fiona simply refused to accept their past relationship had been nothing but sex.

She *had* loved him. She knew she had. No one made the kind of sacrifice she'd made except out of a deep and true love!

Satisfied at long last, she glanced up from where she'd been blankly looking at the menu which the very discreet waiter had left with her some time back.

Philip was silently studying the wine list, looking incredibly serious and incredibly handsome. She let herself admire him for a few secret moments, before glancing around again.

'What a perfect setting for a restaurant,' she said. 'I presume you come here often, Philip?'

He looked up from the wine list and she smiled over at him, determined to act naturally. His head cocked slightly to one side and she could see his mind ticking away.

Fiona wondered what he was thinking.

'Often enough,' he returned. 'It's one of the places I can have a few glasses of wine with my dinner and not have to worry about driving home afterwards. I can walk.'

'You always did like your wine,' she murmured, the comment sparking another memory, which contradicted something Philip had said earlier.

'You know, we *did* talk back then, Philip,' she pointed out, before she could think better of it. 'Especially in the beginning. Remember the first night you took me out? To that fancy restaurant in town? You ordered a bottle of wine and I was scandalised by the price. We sat at that table till the restaurant closed, just talking. You talked to me about everything under the sun. Remember?'

He smiled a rather rueful smile. 'Of course I remember. Only too well. I was trying to impress you, with the wine *and* the conversation.'

'Then you succeeded.'

'Really?'

She bristled at his cynical tone. 'Yes, Philip. *Really.*'

'I doubt it would be as easy to impress you these days. So, what would you like to drink, Fiona?' he asked when the waiter materialised once again by their table. 'I can't drink much, not if I'm going to drive afterwards. Maybe a glass or two.'

'Perhaps we could share a bottle,' she suggested.

'White or red?'

'White,' she returned firmly. 'Chardonnay. Oaked.'

One of his eyebrows arched, and he handed her the wine list. '*You* choose, then,' he commanded.

She hesitated only a fraction before dropping her eyes to the list and swiftly selecting a Tasmanian Chardonnay which she'd never tried before but which was hopefully as good as its price warranted. She ordered it in a crisp, confident voice, handing the wine list back to the waiter before returning a steady gaze to Philip.

He was watching her with a type of reluctant admiration.

'I see you really know your wines nowadays,' he said, once they were alone again.

Fiona shrugged. 'There are a lot of things I know nowadays that I didn't once.'

He leant back in his chair and gave her a long, thoughtful look. 'Yes, I can see that. And I have to admit I'm curious. How did you go from being Noni to Fiona? It's more than just a surface transformation. You do everything differently. The way you walk and talk. The way you dress and do your make-up. Everything, really. It couldn't have come easily, or cheaply.'

'It didn't.'

'So who paid for the transformation? Alimony from

your truck driver ex? Or some sugar daddy you met after your divorce?'

Fiona frowned. He really did have a low opinion of her. 'I'll have you know I paid for everything with money I earned myself. The modelling school. The elocution classes. Endless night school. Everything.'

'Doing what, exactly?'

'My Higher School Certificate, for starters. How long do you think *that* took?'

'That's not what I meant, although I'm sure it didn't take you all that long. You always were very smart, even if you didn't think so yourself. I meant how did you earn the money for all those courses? That couldn't have been easy.'

'I worked in a factory packing meat during the week and as a waitress at the weekend. At a wedding reception place. That's where I learnt a lot about the wedding business. Owen worked there, too, actually. He—'

The return of the waiter with the wine had Fiona breaking off her story mid-stream. She nodded her approval when he went through the charade of presenting the bottle to her with the label on show, then sat there silently while he opened it and poured out a small amount for her to sample.

She sipped it, said it was fine, then waited again—somewhat impatiently—while both their glasses were skilfully filled and the bottle was arranged in the portable ice bucket. She was eager to get back to telling Philip all she'd achieved on her own. She'd liked the way he'd started watching her while she spoke, with respect and admiration, much better than his thinking she was some kind of slut who had slept her way to success.

'Would you like to order yet, Mr Forsythe?' the waiter checked before he left the table.

Fiona was pleased when Philip told him to come back in a couple of minutes, then turned his attention back to her, leaning forward slightly and looking deeply into her eyes.

'Go on,' he said warmly. 'You were saying something about Owen working there as well?'

'Yes. He was responsible for the table setting and the flowers. Owen's very creative. He also worked at a formal clothes hire place during the week. His mother was a professional dressmaker and taught him a lot about clothes, especially wedding clothes. They were her specialty. We used to have coffee together after a reception was over and talk about our plans for the future. I told Owen I wanted to go into PR work and he said he was going to open a wedding consultancy. Once we realised both careers complemented each other, we started working towards going into business together. I found work at an established wedding consultancy to learn the ropes and we both started saving madly. In less than a year, Five-Star Weddings became a reality. I don't think I'm boasting when I say we've been very successful.'

'Amazing. Your dad must be very proud of you.'

'Er...not exactly. We don't see each other any more.'

'Why's that?'

Fiona sighed. 'He wasn't pleased about my leaving Kevin for starters. On top of that, he finally found himself a new wife, and Doreen doesn't care for me at all. She thinks I'm too la-di-da. So does Dad now.' She smiled a sad smile. 'Weird, isn't it? Your mother once called me cheap and common. Now my own father calls me a snob. You can't win, can you?'

'That reminds me,' Philip said, frowning and straightening up.

'Reminds you of what?'

'Of that question I wanted to ask you…'

Fiona tensed, and Philip threw her a searching look.

'The night of our wedding…'

The vice around Fiona's chest tightened further. 'What about it?'

'Remember when the doctor left and Mum sent me down the road to get the painkillers he prescribed?'

'Y…yes…'

'Did Mum say anything to you while I was gone? Put any pressure on you to give up on our marriage so quickly? I mean…from what you said yesterday, her criticisms affected you even more than I realised at the time. I've been wondering if she used some kind of emotional blackmail, or maybe even a bribe to get you to—'

'A *bribe*!' Fiona broke in, shocked and angry. 'You think I took *money* from your mother to leave you?'

His face remained unmoved. 'It crossed my mind, Fiona. It's just that you seemed to change radically while I was away. One minute you were clinging to me and crying over our lost baby. Then, half an hour later, you'd gone all cold on me. You could hardly even look at me as you told me of your decision to call it quits with our marriage and our relationship. It's only reasonable to wonder whether Mother might have got to you while I was away.'

'I didn't even *speak* to your mother that night. I couldn't bear to look at her for thinking how relieved she must be that my baby was gone.'

He nodded slowly, sadly. 'I see. Well, I just had to be sure.'

'Please, Philip,' she said shakily, eyes pleading. 'Can we close that subject once and for all?'

He frowned. 'It still upsets you?'

'Of course it still upsets me. I lost my baby that day. I don't like to think about it.'

His frown deepened. 'Is that why you decided not to have any more children? Because you're frightened that might happen again?'

Fiona could feel her emotions getting the better of her. To break down in front of Philip at this stage would be disastrous! She had to be strong. And hard. She hadn't survived this long to weaken now.

'It wasn't children I decided against so much, but marriage. And I don't believe in having children outside of marriage. Not for any moralistic reason but because I think children need two parents, married and in love, to have the best chance of growing up to be well-adjusted adults instead of needy neurotics.'

'And is that what you think *you* are? A needy neurotic?'

'Sometimes. Oh, good, here's the waiter. Now, what shall I order…?'

Ordering their courses was nicely distracting. Unfortunately, the waiter soon bustled off to do their bidding, leaving Fiona alone with Philip once more. She had never felt more strained in all her life. How she was going to get through the next couple of hours she had no idea!

She could not bear to talk about the past any more. She could not bear to look at him and think of all those wonderful times they'd spent together.

She was, indeed, neurotic and needy. Maybe she always had been.

'Have you chosen your best man?' she said abruptly into the awkward silence which had descended on their table.

Philip stiffened in his chair. 'Why?'

'I'll need to take both of you along to the formal wear place and order your suits soon. In fact, best we do that one day next week. There's this place in town I always recommend because they have the biggest and widest range of clothes, but they might still have to order something in your sizes. Do you want to hire or buy?'

Philip's expression was worrying.

'What is it?' she asked. 'What's wrong?'

'My best man,' he said. 'It's Steve.'

'Steve from university?'

'Uh-huh.'

Steve had been a regular at the fish and chip shop in Newtown where she'd worked ten years ago. It was popular with students because it was close to the campus and the food was cheap and filling. It had been Steve who'd brought Philip into the shop, telling his friend that the girl behind the counter was a real honey.

When Philip had left the shop with a date with Noni for that night, Steve had been a bit jealous. He'd fancied her as well.

Fiona sighed. This was getting far too complicated. 'Does he *have* to be your best man?'

'He's my best friend. And I've already asked him.'

Fiona picked up her wine and took a deep swallow.

'He probably won't recognise you,' Philip went on.

'But if he does, I'll tell him the truth. He won't let on to anyone if I ask him not to.'

'He doesn't fancy Corinne, or anything, does he?'

'Good God, no! Why do you say that?'

'Because he once fancied me, that's why?'

'Ahh, I see. Well, he doesn't fancy Corinne. Fact is, I don't think he cares for Corinne at all.'

Fiona was surprised. 'Why's that?' she asked.

'I'm not sure. Neither was Steve when I questioned him. But Steve has a narrow view of the opposite sex. He likes his women on the obvious side.'

'Well, thank you very much for the compliment!'

'Come now, Fiona, you have to admit you were once a very sexy piece of goods.'

'Not any more.'

He wiggled his hand as though that was a fifty-fifty proposition. 'Wear what you wore on Sunday for the clothes fitting next week and Steve won't take too much notice. Wear the little number you've got on today and his tongue will be on the floor.'

Fiona tried to take offence, but she couldn't. The image was too funny and she laughed. 'Maybe I will, then, if Steve's as handsome as he once was. But what about *your* tongue? I didn't notice it on the floor to-day.'

'It's not my tongue I'm worried about.'

Fiona's eyes widened. 'I thought you said you didn't find me attractive any more.'

'Don't start flirting with me, Fiona,' he warned sharply. 'Keep that side of yourself for the Marks of this world. And don't go making eyes at Steve, either. He's on the look-out for a wife, and I don't think you quite fill the bill, do you?'

'I'll try to control myself,' she said tartly.

'Do that.'

The entrée arrived, and Fiona set about spooning the spicy stir-fry concoction into her mouth and washing the dish down with great gulps of the wine. When her head started spinning, she stopped both the eating and drinking.

Philip looked up from where he'd been devouring a dozen oysters. 'Something wrong with your entrée?'

'No. I'm just not used to eating much lunch. And you make one crack about my weight and you're a dead man!'

'Wouldn't dream of it. I can see today you're not quite as thin as I thought. Maybe it's the lack of underwear.'

Fiona glanced down, horrified to see that her jacket had parted and the black satin camisole had pulled tight across her bustline, outlining her braless breasts. Gritting her teeth, she yanked the jacket closed and did the button up at the waist.

'Don't do that on my account,' Philip said drily. 'I was enjoying the view.'

'You men are all the same,' Fiona accused.

'Mark likes you without underwear, too?'

'I am *not* without underwear,' she snapped, her face flaming at this reminder of the times she hadn't worn any for him. 'Stop embarrassing me.'

'Sorry.'

'No, you're not! You're not at all! Which just shows how wrong I was about you yesterday.'

'Concerning what?'

'I thought you hadn't changed much, except that you were even better-looking. But I see now that you *have* changed. And not for the better! You've grown hard, Philip. Hard and cynical.'

'Have I indeed? Well, people do change, Fiona. You only have to look in the mirror to know that.'

'That's the kind of remark I'm beginning to expect from you.'

'Really?' He dabbed at his mouth with the white serviette and pushed away his plate. 'Then I'll try to curb my cynical tongue and be more polite in future.'

'Do that.'

One waiter arrived to whisk away their plates while another refilled their glasses.

'Shall we drink to a truce?' Philip suggested, and raised his glass towards her.

'Only if you mean to honour it. And only if it covers all my requirements of behaviour.'

He returned his glass to the table. 'Perhaps you could outline what kind of behaviour you require.'

'Very well. We will be polite to each other at all times, even when alone. We will not bring up the past again. We will not say anything sarcastic or do anything to cause each other embarrassment from this moment till you leave on your honeymoon.'

'Mmm. A tall order.'

'Pretend we've only just met!'

He laughed. 'Now that's downright impossible.'

'*Try*. Think of it as a personal challenge.'

'A challenge, Fiona? More like a test of human endurance.' He raised his glass, his sardonic smile sending a strangely erotic shiver down her spine.

'Very well. To Fiona's truce,' he toasted.

Fiona almost reluctantly raised her glass and clinked it against his. Philip stared at her hard, put the glass to his lips and tipped the rest of the wine down his throat.

CHAPTER TEN

OWEN must have been listening for her return, because
the moment Fiona walked in—alone—shortly after
three, he made an appearance, his face showing some
concern.

'So how did it go?' he asked anxiously as he followed her down the corridor and into her office. 'Do
we still have the job?'

Fiona placed her handbag on her desk, extracted a
cheque from its depths and handed it to him. 'Take a
gander at that!'

Owen did, gaping. 'But that's more than *twice* what
we've ever charged for a wedding before!' he exclaimed.

'Natch. This will be our most lavish wedding so far.
And we're being paid double the fee, remember?'

Owen was still staring down at the cheque. 'But
he's paid the lot, up front. Is the man mad? I thought
he was a lawyer.'

'I don't think this money means much to him. It's
probably inherited.'

'What's the difference? Money's money, isn't it?'
Owen said, and kissed the cheque. 'I'm going to run
down and put this in the bank straight away. You're
brilliant, Fiona! Bloody brilliant!' And he raced out.

Fiona sighed deeply and walked over to close the
door. Briefly, she leant against it, her eyes closing, her
heart sinking.

Brilliant, was she?

More like stupid.

After the truce had been toasted to, things had relaxed a bit between them. They'd managed to chat over the main course without argument, though they'd kept to innocuous subjects like Sydney's recent water supply problems, plus the coming election.

Still, it had not been unpleasant. And quite satisfying in a way to show that she was now a well-informed woman with intelligent opinions of her own.

Of course, the absence of any sarcasm on Philip's part had helped, plus the four glasses of wine she'd downed by then. When it had come time for dessert Fiona had felt quite mellow, and she'd given in to Philip's cajolery to try the soufflé of the day, which had turned out to be butterscotch.

Fiona had always adored anything which smacked of caramel or butterscotch flavour.

The soufflé had been mouthwateringly scrumptious, Philip laughing when she'd oohed and ahhed her way all through it. The relaxed warmth of his laughter had been disarming, and charming.

By the time coffee had come Fiona had let down her guard so much that when Philip had started telling her about a murder case he'd been recently hired to defend, she'd been powerless to resist what she'd always found his most irresistible attraction.

His passion.

She had soon been engrossed, leaning her elbows on the table whilst she sipped her coffee and listened intently to his rich, male voice.

His defendant was a woman, a housewife in her late forties, who had hit her husband over the head with one of his golf clubs and killed him. Apparently, she wanted to plead guilty, but Philip had discovered a history of emotional and physical abuse which would have driven anyone to strike back eventually. He wanted her to plead temporary insanity but the poor woman had been horrified.

When Fiona had suggested that a self-defence plea might go down better, both with the defendant herself and the jury, Philip had become quite excited.

'You're right,' he'd exclaimed, blue eyes gleaming. 'Self-defence is much better. Much more real and sympathetic. You're brilliant, Fiona.'

After that, he'd become very animated, outlining the new strategies he would employ, what witnesses he had, and the arguments he would use. Fiona had just sat there, listening, and almost envying the woman, having Philip as her champion. For she knew he would never let her down.

He hadn't let *her* down ten years ago, she'd begun thinking. From the moment she'd told him of her pregnancy he'd been there for her, insisting she not worry, reassuring her that he loved her and that they would be married.

It had hit her forcibly at that moment that maybe she'd been wrong all those years ago to give Philip up. Maybe his *father* had been wrong.

Maybe her sacrifice *had* all been for nothing!

She'd suddenly felt very upset, and had had to struggle to hide her feelings, sitting up straight and trying not to look perturbed. Philip must have sensed something, because he'd stopped talking about the case and abruptly called for the bill.

Later, in the car, his voice had been brusque. 'Sorry for boring you back then. We men do like to talk about ourselves, especially when we think we've got an interested audience. I forgot you were only there under sufferance.'

Fiona had hardly been in a position to deny any of his assumptions. What could she have said? I *was* interested. *Too* interested.

'I won't have time to come up to your office when we get back,' he'd swept on. 'I'm meeting Corinne to buy the rings. I'll write you a cheque for your fee. If you still insist on a contract, then you can bring it with you next week, when we meet to order the suits. Tell me when and where for that, and Steve and I'll be there.'

She had. She'd also not argued when he'd written that outrageous cheque and given it to her, saying curtly, 'That should cover everything.'

It surely would, she thought as she levered herself away from the door and walked wearily back to her desk. And a contract was hardly necessary, once the cheque was cleared.

Fiona slumped down behind her desk, too depressed to even cry. Work was impossible.

So was going out with Mark tonight, she finally realised. How could she sit there with him in that restaurant, thinking of Philip? And how could she possibly go to bed with him afterwards, wishing he *was* Philip?

It wasn't fair to Mark, for one thing, which was something she hadn't considered much before now. She'd really become a selfish cow when it came to men. Owen was right. She used them. Not just for the sex, though she could not deny she did have strong needs in that area. Sometimes she went to bed with a man simply for a pair of strong arms to hold her through the night and take away the aching loneliness in her empty heart.

Philip's return had changed the ball game, however. Suddenly, her heart was full again. To overflowing.

Unfortunately.

Fiona reached for the phone and did what had to be done.

Mark didn't take the news well, which made her feel even worse. He demanded to know the identity of the man who was going to take his place in her bed. In a warped kind of way, he seemed to *want* there to be someone else. He could not believe she was simply breaking up with him because she didn't want to see him any more. He was so insistent that in the end Fiona cracked and gave him what he wanted.

'Oh, all right,' she bit out. 'Yes, I've met someone else. An old flame. We ran into each recently and, well…sparks just flew.'

'I knew it,' Mark muttered, still sounding very put out.

'Look, I'm sorry, Mark,' she said, because she *was*. 'I really liked you.' *Once upon a time.* 'But the truth is Philip and I were once married and we—'

'Married!' he squawked.

'Yes, married. We were very young at the time, and things just didn't work out. But from the moment I saw him again I knew I wasn't over him.'

'I see. So you're telling me you're still in love with this man. You have been all along?'

'I'm not sure I would go that far,' Fiona had to concede. 'But I could easily fall in love with him again.'

'I see,' Mark said sourly. 'I wish you'd been more honest with me sooner.'

Fiona only just refrained from telling him she'd always been honest with him. She'd never led him on to believe she loved him, or would ever marry him. But she apologised again, in deference to his obviously battered ego.

'I doubt you're sorry at all!' Mark snapped back. 'But I don't intend losing any sleep over you. If I'm brutally honest, you're not quite what I'm looking for in a wife, anyway. You're far too ambitious, Fiona. And far too selfish. A doctor's wife needs to be able to put her husband first. I can't see you ever putting any man's wishes above your own.'

Not yours anyway, she thought, without a shred of sympathy left for the man.

'So this is a permanent goodbye, I take it?' he actually had the stupidity to ask.

'Yes.' The word had a razor's edge.

'We could continue on a strictly sexual basis, if you like.'

He was lucky she didn't laugh. 'I don't think so, Mark.'

'No point in my hanging around waiting for you to change your mind, then. If nothing else, you're a decisive woman, Fiona. Maybe too decisive. You don't leave a man much room to move sometimes. And you don't leave him much damned pride.' And he slammed the phone down in her ear.

Fiona stared at the dead phone in her hand before slamming the phone down herself. How she'd gone out with such an overblown over-opinionated person in the first place she had no idea!

It was because you were lonely, you idiot, came back the brutal answer. And now you're going to be even lonelier. In fact, if you keep this up, you'll be right back to where you started ten years ago, with your heart breaking over Philip and your life in tatters.

Fiona straightened suddenly and gritted her teeth. No way, she resolved bitterly. Not again!

She wasn't in love with Philip yet, she told herself firmly. It was a sexual attraction, that was all. And admiration. The man was worth admiring.

Love, however, was something quite different. It was a huge investment of one's emotions. It wasn't something which happened overnight, or over one miserable lunch. It took much more time and much more intimacy, neither of which, thankfully, she would be investing with Philip this time.

She would only see him a couple more times before the wedding, for starters. To help with his clothes, and then for the final rehearsal. The wedding didn't count, because even though she would physically see him on that day she wouldn't be talking to him. Certainly not alone, anyway.

And then he'd be off on his honeymoon with Corinne and she could go back to living her own life as it had been before Owen forced her into this ghastly position. She would eventually find herself another man to date. One who wasn't so taken up with himself, and one who wouldn't remind her in any way whatsoever of Philip. Another truck driver perhaps!

The telephone ringing stopped her slightly hysterical self-lecture. She hadn't realised how crazy she was sounding. How darned infantile!

Because of course she only ever dated men who reminded her in some way of Philip. Sometimes it was a pair of intelligent blue eyes, or a way of walking, or talking, or dressing. Damn Philip, she thought savagely. He'd ruined her for any other man!

The phone kept on jangling, demanding an answer. She swept the darned thing up, punching out her name in a crisp businesslike fashion.

'Hi, there, Fiona,' came the very breezy reply. 'It's Corinne here. Philip's just been telling me you had such a lovely lunch together, and I'm simply frightfully jealous. All that scrummy food!'

Fiona pressed her lips firmly together and breathed in and out deeply behind them. She wasn't in the mood for sweetness at that moment, or for Corinne at all!

'Yes, it was very nice,' she only just managed.

'I'm going to make him take me down to that restaurant very, very soon. He's always talking about it but we never seem to get there together.'

Fiona could not help feeling perversely glad about that. Another futile feeling, but there you are!

'He also said you'd lined up a date to fix him and Stevie up with suits for the wedding.'

Fiona winced slightly at the 'Stevie'. She was always irritated by girls who added unnecessary 'e's to the ends of names and words. In truth, she wasn't sure she could take too much of Corinne. There was only just so much sugar she could swallow.

'Have you decided what they're going to wear yet?' Corinne added brightly.

'I thought I would leave that up to Philip.'

'Well, just between us girls, Fiona, please don't let them wear one of those awful tails outfits. Those ones with the grey jackets and top hats. I would simply hate Philip in one of those silly hats. Grey is *not* a favourite colour of mine. Philip looks absolutely gorgeous in a tux, though. Black, of course. I simply adore black.'

'You're the bride, Corinne. Whatever you want. Just tell Philip.'

'Oh, he'll do whatever you suggest, Fiona. I can see he's very impressed with you. But not as impressed as his mother. She rang me this morning and simply raved some more.'

'Really?'

'I think she wanted to reassure me before I go away, but truly, I don't need reassuring. I have every faith in Philip's judgement of a person, and he says he has no doubt you won't leave a stone unturned to make our wedding a success. Now, speaking of the wedding, I was wondering if Carmel and I could meet you at the first salon you planned on taking us to tomorrow, rather than you picking us up at my place. It would be less trouble for you.'

'It's no trouble, Corinne.' Fiona had found things always went more smoothly if everyone was in one car, since they would probably be traipsing all over Sydney all day.

'Maybe, but Carmel and I want to have our own wheels, if you don't mind, Fiona. So we'll definitely be meeting you there. At ten, you said? I just need the name of the place and the address.'

Fiona was slightly taken aback by the abrupt change from the bubbly and very agreeable Corinne to this coolly assertive version.

Startled, Fiona told her the name and address of the bridal salon in question, after which the girl hung up just as abruptly, leaving Fiona feeling slightly put out. She replaced the phone with a frown on her face.

If Philip's fiancée subscribed to the theory of getting more with honey than with vinegar, then she really should learn not to let the act drop all of a sudden, even if she was only talking to a hireling.

The word 'act' just sprang into Fiona's mind, unbidden. But it immediately began to bother her.

Was this what Steve sensed about Corinne? That she was acting; that she wasn't sincere; that she didn't really love Philip?

Suddenly, meeting Corinne tomorrow took on an added aspect, rather than just getting a job done and perhaps satisfying her curiosity over what Corinne looked like. She now wanted to know what Corinne was actually *like*. Because, darn it all, she wasn't about to sit back and let Philip waste his life on anyone less than the best!

Because that was why she'd given Philip up. For him to have the best in life. And the best in life certainly wasn't some female who didn't truly really love him with every fibre of her being.

Fiona knew what such a love felt like, and if she didn't see the same kind of adoration in Corinne then she would…she would…

Do what? a cynical voice inserted.

God only knew.

But she sure as hell would do *something*!

CHAPTER ELEVEN

THE bridal salon was just off the Pacific Highway, in the northern suburb of Lindfield. It carried a wide range of wedding dresses, locally made gowns alongside those imported from Asia and America, plus every accessory imaginable, from veils to shoes, underwear to jewellery. It was a one-stop shop for busy brides, and was always Fiona's first port of call when looking for a wedding dress off the rack.

Fiona slid her Audi into the kerb outside the shop ten minutes before the allotted time for meeting Corinne and Carmel, cut the engine and just sat there, waiting. It was a fine sunny morning, but somewhat on the fresh side. Pleasant enough, though, provided you stayed in the car.

Fiona stayed in the car, thinking.

At five past ten a zappy little red sports car pulled in behind and two girls got out, laughing.

Fiona studied them in the rearview mirror for a few unobserved moments. The driver was very tall, with an athletic figure and short brown hair. The passenger had long straight blonde hair, and was of medium height, with a shapely hour-glass figure. Both girls were wearing jeans and sweaters. Both wore sunglasses, which prevented Fiona from seeing if they were really pretty or not, but from what she could see the word 'unattractive' did not spring to mind. She hadn't thought it would.

Fiona climbed out from behind the wheel and

walked over to where the two girls were standing, gazing up at the bridal mannequin in the shop window and making comments.

'That would suit you, Cori,' the brunette was saying. 'Especially with your gorgeous boobs.'

Fiona had already noticed the gorgeous boobs herself. And the girl was right. The dress in the window, with its low heart-shaped neckline, tight lace bodice and flouncy tulle skirt, would show the blonde's figure off to perfection.

'Hello,' she said a little stiffly from just behind them. 'You must be Corinne and Carmel. I'm Fiona.'

Corinne turned and looked Fiona up and down. She whipped off her sunglasses, and whistled. 'Wow, Fiona. Philip forgot to tell me how gorgeous you were!'

It seemed 'gorgeous' was the in word with these two.

Fiona, who'd dressed down for the occasion in brown, knew she didn't look at all gorgeous that morning. Sleepless nights did that to one.

But she accepted the flattery with a polite if somewhat plastic smile, told herself that she wasn't crushed that Corinne's eyes were like emerald pools, and set about trying to discover if Philip's fiancée was a genuine *ingénue*, or a callous, cold-blooded creature who was only marrying Philip for his money, or some such other equally superficial reason.

'Don't you think Fiona's gorgeous, Carmel?' Corinne said, and nudged her bridesmaid in the ribs.

Carmel, who'd also taken off her sunglasses, gave Fiona a sour glance and declined to comment. She wasn't nearly as pretty as her friend, her black eyes spoiled by heavy eyelids which gave her a sulky, sullen look.

Fiona decided it matched her disposition. She wondered what someone as effervescent as Corinne was doing with her, unless it was because Carmel made her look good by comparison. She'd known other stunning girls with vibrant personalities with the oddest friends.

'Shall we go inside?' Fiona suggested, uncaring and unbothered by Carmel's rudeness. It was the bride's true character she wanted to uncover.

Unfortunately, Corinne remained on her best and most delightful behaviour all morning, and, as much as Fiona hated to admit it, she didn't put a foot wrong. For once, she showed some interest in the wedding—or at least in what she was going to wear—continuously asking Carmel whether she thought Philip would like her in whatever gown she was trying on at the time.

On one occasion it tartly crossed Fiona's mind that Corinne would have been better off asking *her*, Philip's ex-wife. But she could hardly say so.

Carmel gave all of the gowns the thumbs-down, except the one from the window, which she said was definitely the one. She sounded sincere too, her cold black eyes lighting up for the first time in over two hours.

Unfortunately, Fiona had to agree. Corinne looked simply delicious in that dress. Philip could not help but be turned on by the sight of her in it. Fiona knew what he liked, and that dress was definitely it—plus the curvaceous body in it.

Fiona only just stopped herself from trying to talk the girl out of buying it.

The dress decided upon, Corinne simply had to ring Philip and tell him. She even borrowed Fiona's mobile to do so.

Fiona just stood there, next to a lemon-faced Carmel, while Corinne gushed and gammered to her beloved over the dress, told him she loved him a thousand times, and how much she was going to miss him while she was away, but how it would be worth the wait when he saw her in that dress.

If it was an act, it was a darned good one. Still, when she started blowing kisses down the line Fiona knew she'd heard enough.

'Let's leave the mobile with Corinne and go find you something in black, Carmel,' she suggested brusquely to the brunette.

'Not without Corinne,' she was promptly told. 'There's no point. I'm here to do what *she* wants, not what *I* want. So are you, aren't you?'

Fiona felt duly chastened, and waited bleakly till Corinne was finished. The blushing bride finally handed back the mobile, her cheeks all pink and rosy.

Fiona gave up at that moment, admitting to herself she'd been grabbing at straws in hoping to find something shallow and nasty about Corinne. When a girl got so excited by a mere phone call then she had to be in love.

'Thanks, Fiona,' Corinne said. 'You're a doll!' She whirled around and admired herself anew in the many mirrors in the salon. 'Don't you just love me in this dress, Carmel?' she said, her face still flushed.

Carmel's mouth tightened a fraction, and it occurred to Fiona that the one and only bridesmaid might be just a little jealous of the bride's beauty. 'It's perfect, Cori,' she said, though her voice was cold.

Corinne smiled at her, then linked arms, pulling a reluctant Carmel to her side. 'Now we have to find something just as smashing for you. Something sleek and slinky and sexy, in black satin.'

Carmel looked doubtful. 'I'm not really the slinky and sexy type, Cori. I don't have the figure for it.'

'Oh, don't be silly. I simply *love* your figure. You're so tall and slim. And you have the best legs in the world. Maybe we could get you a dress which has a slit up the side to show them off. What do you think, Fiona?'

Fiona prayed for patience. She was going to need every drop she possessed, and more, to get through this day. 'Let's go and see what they have in stock in black satin, shall we?'

'Yes, let's. Oh, this is much more fun than I thought it would be!'

Fiona only just stopped herself rolling her eyes.

Thankfully, they found a black satin gown for Carmel which looked, if not sexy and slinky, then coolly elegant on the girl. It was a simple enough sheath, with a bow at the back and, yes, a slit up one of the sides. She needed it to be able to walk.

Black certainly did suit her, Fiona thought as she stood back and looked at the pair.

'The black and white does look good together,' she conceded. 'Did Kathryn tell you about the idea I had for the guests, Corinne? She said she would.'

'You mean about everyone wearing black and white? Yes, she did, and I think it's positively brilliant! Sydney's had plenty of black and white balls, but never a strictly black and white wedding that I recall. All the women guests will be rushing to the boutiques, snapping up all the black and white ball-gowns. How on earth did you think of it?'

'It just came to me,' Fiona said. She declined to tell her that with such a small wedding party and an at-home reception she'd had to think of something to make the wedding stand out in people's minds. Owen would be very disappointed if Five-Star Weddings didn't get *some* mileage out of this.

'By the way, Corinne,' Fiona went on, 'Kathryn mentioned Philip has a couple of young cousins who would make the perfect page-boy and flower girl. I know you don't want any more bridesmaids, but I didn't think you'd mind that.'

'No, I don't mind that at all. What will they do, exactly?'

'The page-boy will carry the ring cushion. He will go first, then Carmel, then the flower girl next, strewing rose petals in your path. Red rose petals, I thought. In fact, I was thinking red roses for both your bouquets and the men's lapels. They would look simply magnificent against all the black and white.'

'They certainly would. Yes.'

'I have a folder of various bouquets in the car,' Fiona told her. 'I'll go get it and you can choose what—'

'Oh, no, don't bother me with that,' Corinne interrupted. '*You* choose.'

Fiona stared at her. Not once, in all the weddings she'd helped with, had she had a bride who didn't want to choose her own bouquet.

Corinne must have seen the look on her face.

The girl's smile was dazzling. 'We just haven't got the time for me to choose everything personally, Fiona, darling. That's why Kathryn hired *you*. And I can understand why. You're so efficient. And you've done it all before so many times. I trust you implicitly to make me into the bride of the year. After all, that's your job, isn't it?'

'Yes,' Fiona returned, feeling a little confused. Was this girl for real or not? 'But it's *your* wedding, Corinne. Brides usually have definite ideas about what they like and don't like.'

'Oh, I have definite ideas about what I like and don't like, don't I, Carmel?' she returned, an edge creeping into her voice. 'I just don't care much about weddings as such. If society didn't dictate you should be married before you have children I wouldn't be getting married to Philip at all. I would simply have had a baby by him.'

Once again, Fiona was taken aback. 'Well…um… lots of girls do that nowadays anyway.'

Corinne laughed. 'Not with a father like mine, they don't. I—'

Carmel tapped Corinne on the arm. 'I think we'd better get out of these dresses, Cori,' she said firmly. 'We don't want to ruin anything at this stage, do we?'

For a moment Corinne looked angry with her friend, then she smiled a wry smile. 'You're right. That would never do.'

'You'd best choose your shoes before you get undressed,' Fiona said. 'And any other accessories you might want.' She could see this would possibly be her only chance to get the bride and the bridesmaid fully outfitted.

In only one added hour all purchases had been made, Corinne and Carmel had driven off together, and Fiona was on her way back to the office, feeling decidedly perturbed.

With any other bride she would have been busy with her all day. And maybe another day as well. But Corinne was clearly not the run-of-the-mill bride. She certainly wasn't the perfect 'She just wants to be Philip's wife and the mother of his children' creature which Kathryn had outlined on Sunday.

Fiona wondered if Philip knew of this unconventional and rebellious side to Corinne, if she'd confided her secret wish not to be married to him but to have his babies out of wedlock.

No, not babies, Fiona amended in her mind with a frown. 'Baby', the girl had said. Did she only want the one? Philip, Fiona was sure, would want more. He had ten years ago. Why would he have changed? Surely Kathryn had intimated as much on Sunday as well. He wanted children, not just the one child. He'd been an only child himself and hated it.

Fiona wasn't in any doubt that the girl loved Philip. But love wasn't enough when you were two totally different people, when you had different goals and different agendas.

Philip and Corinne seemed the perfect couple on the surface, but were they? Would Corinne make Philip happy if she didn't really want the constriction of marriage? Surely it was an indictment of her character that she was flitting off overseas during the weeks leading up to the wedding. Her outer gaiety might well be a cover for an inner restlessness. Why couldn't Philip see that?

Worse, what could Fiona possibly do about it?

She could hardly ring Philip up and tell him her theories about Corinne. Neither was there any point in saying anything to Kathryn when they met later this week to finalise everything for the wedding. Philip's mother thought the sun shone out of Corinne. Which it did, in a way. The girl had an irresistible and radiant charm when she chose to exercise it.

A thought suddenly crossed Fiona's mind.

Steve. The best man.

It seemed Steve didn't care for Corinne. She would be seeing Steve next Tuesday, to kit him and Philip out for the wedding.

Fiona would keep her eyes and ears open, and if an opportunity presented itself she would…she would…

Well, she wasn't sure what she would do. But she would do something! She couldn't stand by and let Philip marry the wrong girl. She'd set him free so that he could be happy. And something—some deep, inner female instinct—was warning her that he would *not* be happy with Corinne!

CHAPTER TWELVE

'AREN'T you supposed to be meeting Philip and his best man in town this morning?' Owen said to her when she walked into the office at eight-thirty the following Tuesday morning.

'Not till eleven,' she replied, her crisp tone belying the butterflies in her stomach. 'I'll catch a train around ten and still be in plenty of time.'

Owen's eyes narrowed and flicked over her mint-green linen suit. 'That's new, isn't it?'

'Yes, it is.' In actuality she'd bought it to wear to some of the spring weddings they were doing. She'd been going to wear grey or brown today, but feminine pride had had the final say that morning. 'Do you like it?'

'You look like a breath of fresh air,' he grumbled.

'And that's bad?'

'Only if you're going to meet your ex.'

'Give that a rest, will you, Owen?'

'I will...after you get back safely with the wedding still on. At least after today you won't need to see Philip again till the week of the wedding.'

Owen's very correct comment reminded Fiona that this morning was her last real opportunity to do something about Corinne.

'That bothers you, does it?' Owen said sharply.

It did, but Fiona tried to look unconcerned.

'Not really. Why?'

'Just checking. My problem antenna is still beeping. It has been ever since we took this job.'

'A job *you* insisted we take, I might add,' Fiona pointed out drily.

'Yeah. Yeah. Don't rub it in. So, how are things really going?'

'Swimmingly. Never had less trouble. What I say goes. I've never known a wedding like it. On top of that, if everything goes off as planned, it really will be something to behold.'

'What do you mean...*if*?'

Fiona didn't seriously believe she could stop this wedding. All she could do was make sure Philip knew what kind of girl he was marrying in advance.

'Oh, you know,' she said airily, then began to walk off. 'There are always things you can't control. Acts of God and such.'

'I'm not worried about acts of God,' Owen called after her. 'It's the acts of the devil which concern me.'

Fiona had to laugh. Did Owen seriously think she was about to seduce the groom? Even if she wanted to—and, yes, she did, in her darker moments—Philip wasn't in the market for seduction. Not by her, anyway.

He'd made it perfectly clear what he thought of her. Perfectly, perfectly clear!

That was why she didn't really feel guilty over wearing her new green outfit. She could stand naked before Philip and she doubted he would turn a hair.

Well...maybe a little hair...

Eleven o'clock saw her standing before the man in question, but, true to form, he was looking at her quite coldly. He was also looking heart-breakingly handsome in a dark grey suit and pale blue shirt.

Steve, however, was nowhere in sight.

'Steve's always late,' Philip said brusquely, glancing at his watch.

'Shall we wait for him?' Fiona asked. They were in the reception area of Formal Wear for Men, which occupied the first floor of a rather old building in King Street, not far from Wynyard Station.

'No, let's not. I don't have that much time. I have a meeting with a client after lunch. We can leave a message for him at Reception.'

They did, and were soon ushered inside the vast showrooms by a dapper-looking salesman who started showing Philip some of the more modern suits grooms were being decked out in these days. Philip stopped him in his tracks before he'd barely begun.

'My fiancée wants me in a black dinner suit,' he stated firmly. 'With a white dress shirt and black bow tie. She's quite adamant about that. So show me what you have in that range.'

'I see. Well, if you and your fiancée would like to come this way…' And he flashed Fiona a warm smile.

Philip shot Fiona a savage glance, which prompted her to inform the man she was *not* the fiancée in question. The salesman looked startled, then apologised for the mistake.

'And there I was, thinking what a handsome couple you would make,' he went on with an embarrassed laugh.

'Fiona's a consultant with Five-Star Weddings,' Philip said stiffly.

'Oh, yes, so she is. I recognise her now.'

After that, Fiona hung back a little while the salesman showed Philip several racks of black tuxedos, pointing out the various styles and shapes.

Philip selected an extremely elegant but traditional dinner suit, with deep black satin lapels and only one button at his waist. He matched it with a fine white shirt which had tiny black buttons and vertical pleats on each side. The bow tie was black too, as Corinne had ordered.

'I'll go try this on,' he informed the man serving him. 'When my best man arrives, I want him dressed exactly the same. And don't even *think* of suggesting one of those ghastly cummerbund things, Fiona. Neither of us would be seen dead in one.'

Philip promptly disappeared into one of the dressing cubicles, which Fiona was glad to see had proper doors. It would be bad enough waiting outside, thinking of him undressing. Much worse if she was able to glimpse bare bits and pieces of him under one of those half-doors.

Fiona sighed as she waited. This wasn't working out at all as she'd hoped. Steve wasn't here, and Philip was so cold and remote that it was impossible to bring up the subject of his bride.

Suddenly the door of the cubicle popped open and Philip leant out. 'I can't do this infernal bow tie up,' he muttered, glancing around for the salesman, who'd unfortunately been grabbed by a large man in a safari suit.

'Fiona,' he finally said in desperation. 'Come in here and do the damned thing up for me.'

Rather reluctantly, she moved into the cubicle, which, though larger than the cramped boxes some shops offered, was still far too small once the door was shut.

And it did shut behind her, operated by one of those

automatic do-dads which shut doors once they were let go.

Fiona tried to act cool, moving round to face Philip and reaching up to do what she'd done a hundred times before. When you organised weddings you learnt to do fiddly things like tie bow ties, and pin roses to lapels. Usually the people in the wedding party were all fingers and thumbs. One of Fiona's main tasks on a wedding day was to provide an un-flustered mind and a steady hand.

But being this close to Philip did something to her mind and her hands. They both ceased to work properly.

Her first attempt at tying the tie was woeful. She gave a shaky laugh at the pathetic sight. 'Sorry,' she muttered, and pulled the ends undone. 'I'll try again.'

She didn't dare look up into his eyes. Instead she stared straight ahead and tried with all her might to tie a proper bow tie.

But once again it ended up all lopsided.

'I…er…think you'll have to get someone else to do this,' she said, somewhat breathlessly.

When he didn't say a single word, she looked up, then desperately wished she hadn't. He was too close. Far, far too close.

His eyes searched hers with a harsh and haunted expression, betraying in that moment that he did still feel something for her.

'Why did you leave me?' he demanded angrily. 'Why, damn you?'

Her heart tightened at the torment in his voice and face, her hand trembling as it reached up to touch his cheek. 'Oh, Philip,' was all she could manage.

He gave no warning of his intention to kiss her;

nothing, except perhaps for a moment's darkening of his eyes. Suddenly his hands shot out to grab her shoulders, she was yanked against him and his mouth crashed down hard upon hers.

Fiona gasped under his lips, an automatic air-seeking reaction which proved fateful.

Did he think she'd parted her lips deliberately, inviting him to drive his tongue deep into her mouth?

He must have, because he immediately pushed her back against the mirrored wall, holding her face captive with his hands while he did just that.

Philip had always been a hungry kisser, but this…this was something else. This was beyond hunger.

Initially, Fiona was stunned by his brutal oral onslaught. Shock, however, soon began to give way to a burst of excitement which was as dangerous as it was reckless. She began kissing him back, her tongue twining round his, her head spinning as the blood roared through her head. He pressed against her, then *rubbed* against her. She whimpered, and writhed.

When he reefed back away from her, she stared up into his flushed face and glittering eyes, then reached blindly out to touch him through his trousers, stroking him to even greater arousal.

'Oh, God,' he groaned.

The banging on the cubicle door had both of their eyes blinking wide.

'Philip! Are you in there?'

Philip stifled another groan and squeezed his eyes tightly shut.

Fiona could not believe how quickly one could go from madness to mortification. One moment she was in the grip of mindless lust, the next she just wanted to die.

Her hand whipped away from his trousers, her face going bright red.

Philip's return to reality was as quick, if a little less inclined to self-disgust. He opened his eyes and speared her with an icily accusing look.

'Yeah, Steve,' he answered curtly. 'I'm in here. Won't be a moment. Fiona's having some trouble doing up my bow tie for me.'

'Who the hell's Fiona?'

'The wedding consultant Corinne and my mother hired.'

'Oh, right. Look, I'm going into the dressing room opposite, okay? I'm trying on the suit you picked out.'

'Fine.'

All the time Philip was talking his coldly furious gaze never left Fiona. As soon as it was obvious Steve was no longer standing outside the door he rounded on her.

'What in hell did you think you were doing, touching me like that?' he demanded.

Fiona was jolted by the unfairness of the attack. 'I…I couldn't help it,' she stammered with uncharacteristic confusion, before pulling herself together. 'Hey, you kissed me first, remember?'

'Only after you touched my face and started looking at me with goo-goo eyes. And what do you mean, you couldn't help it?' he lashed out. 'What kind of lame excuse is that? What are you? Some kind of nymphomaniac that you can't keep your hands off a man once you come within three feet of him?'

'Don't be ridiculous! I'm nothing of the kind. Not normally, anyway,' she muttered.

'Oh, only with me, is that it? God, that would be funny if it wasn't so pathetic. Why don't you admit it, Fiona? You're sex-mad. You always were and you still are.'

'Sex had nothing to do with why I touched you in the beginning.'

He laughed. 'Well, believe me, honey, sex had everything to with the way you *ended* up touching me.'

'That was only after things got out of hand,' she countered, her face flaming. 'And who are you to accuse me of being sex-mad? You kissed me first. And it wasn't a polite, platonic kiss, either. So what are *you*, Philip?' she countered heatedly. 'Some kind of sex maniac that you can't keep your hands off a woman once you come within three feet of her?'

'Only with you, Fiona,' came his rueful confession. 'Only with you.

'Old memories, I guess,' he went on, before she could take any pleasure in the admission. 'But they're damned powerful old memories. Powerful and perverse. If Steve hadn't knocked when he did, I'd have let you have your wicked way with me. Yep, I admit it. I'd have joined your long line of male victims for a second sick run around your block.'

He gave a short, harsh bark of laughter. 'Hell, I'm only now beginning to appreciate why I had such trouble forgetting you, Fiona. But I'm warning you, honey. You keep well away from me. You had your chance ten years ago, and you blew it. I love Corinne now and I'm going to marry her.'

'Yes, but does *she* love *you*?' Fiona threw back at him, stung by his scorn and his anger.

Philip's eyes showed utter disbelief, then contempt. 'I want you out of here,' he muttered, low under his breath. 'Right now. And I don't want to see hide nor hair of you again till my wedding day, and then only if strictly necessary. Do I make myself clear?'

Fiona saw the bitter resolve in his face and knew she'd lost any chance she'd had. To say any more would be futile, and possibly even more disastrous.

But she simply could not leave without saying something!

'I know you won't believe this, Philip,' she tried to explain, her voice softly pleading, 'but I do care about you. I only had your best interests at heart in saying what I just said. I've only *ever* had your best interests at heart.'

His eyes stayed hard and cold. 'Then you have a funny way of showing it. Now, will you just go, please?'

She still lingered. 'What…what about your suits for the wedding? Owen will ask me, that's all.'

'Tell Owen the groom's taking care of his and the best man's clothes. He exonerates you entirely of the responsibility.'

Fiona winced at his coldness. 'I…I am truly sorry, Philip.'

His mouth tightened. 'Please, just go.'

She gave him one last despairing look, and went.

CHAPTER THIRTEEN

'OH, FIONA, how lovely you look! My, doesn't white suit you! You should wear it more often.'

Fiona's heart tightened. Kathryn had no idea of the irony within her words, or the pain she'd once given Fiona on another wedding day, ten long years ago.

'White's not a very serviceable colour for a career girl,' Fiona replied. 'Neither is this hairdo,' she added wryly, and took another peek in the mirror at the way Kathryn had talked Fiona into having her hair done that morning. Up, with wispy bits hanging down around her face and neck.

'You need a romantic hairdo to go with that romantic dress,' Kathryn had insisted.

The dress was, indeed, romantic. White chiffon, it was an elegant and close-fitting sheath in an off-the-shoulder style, with a self-made rose between her breasts, out of which chiffon scarves floated down to the hem. The neckline wasn't low enough to be vulgar, but it felt bare, so Fiona had added a pearl choker and earrings.

The dress had been an impulse buy, Kathryn steering her in its direction the day she'd taken Philip's mother shopping for her mother-of-the-groom dress. Fiona now thought wryly that she should have bought something black to signify mourning.

Instead, here she was, on Philip's wedding day, looking exquisitely soft and feminine and, yes, sort of bridal.

'I want to thank you for staying here with me last night, dear,' Kathryn was saying. 'I'd have been a bit lonely without anyone.'

Fiona snapped out of her thoughts to smile at Philip's mother. 'It was kind of you to ask me.' She'd grown to genuinely like the woman, which she supposed was perverse in the extreme. But it was true.

Staying overnight hadn't been any great hardship either, since neither Philip nor Corinne was in residence. Philip had spent his last evening of bachelorhood at his best man's place, and Corinne had stayed at home, saying she wanted to have her hair done at her usual hairdresser's in the morning. Fiona presumed Carmel had stayed with her and was going to the same hairdresser.

Both girls were due to drive out to Kenthurst after lunch, arriving around three, giving them four hours to be ready for the wedding, which was scheduled for seven. Their dresses were already hanging up in the guest suite Kathryn had allotted for the bride to use. Philip and Steve weren't due to arrive till the last minute.

Fiona had instructed the parents of the page-boy and flower girl to dress them in their respective homes and keep them there as long as possible as well. Little children, she'd found, were notorious for getting excited and having accidents on wedding days, especially where a staircase was involved, not to mention flagged steps and swimming pools.

The actual ceremony was to take place at one end of the pool, between the marble columns, with the garden as backdrop. Rows of red chairs had been set up on the two sides of the pool and down at the other end for the two-hundred-odd guests. Unfortunately, nearly all those invited had accepted. There'd even been a few last-minute additions, as Corinne's father had thought of some influential people he'd forgotten.

After the ceremony, most of the red chairs would be cleared away, leaving room for dancing around the pool. Not much room for that in the marquee, which sat on the lawn just beyond the terrace and which, though large, was chock-full of tables and chairs for the formal sit-down dinner.

'I hope everything goes smoothly,' Fiona said, giving in to a quite uncharacteristic burst of uncertainty.

Kathryn looked surprised. 'I'm sure it will,' she soothed. 'The weather's marvellous and everything looks just magnificent. The house. The marquee. The lights. Everything! You're just worried because you weren't here the other night for the rehearsal. But, truly, your partner put everyone through their paces without a hitch. Which reminds me. Are you sure you're feeling one hundred per cent better now? I must say you *look* well.'

'I'm fine. It was just one of those twenty-four-hour viruses.' Owen was the only one who knew she hadn't really been sick that day.

Other than Philip, of course.

Fiona hadn't told Owen the whole truth, just that there was a bit of tension building between her and Philip and it would be better all round if he conducted the rehearsal. Owen had been only too glad to oblige. He didn't want anything to spoil the wedding of the year!

Kathryn patted Fiona's hand. 'Corinne was worried you might not make it for the wedding, but Philip was sure you'd be here.'

Fiona winced inside. So he was still angry with her.

What was he thinking? That she might still try to spoil something?

She sighed, and Kathryn gave her a closer look. 'Come to think of it, you *are* a bit pale. How about we go downstairs and have us both a stiff brandy?'

Fiona smiled. 'Good idea, Kathryn.'

The brandy worked. So did keeping busy.

Corinne and Carmel arrived shortly after lunch, and were bustled upstairs with instructions to be ready for the photographer a good hour and a half before the ceremony.

Things really started hopping after that. The flowers were delivered. The video man arrived, keen to get set up well before mingling guests made things difficult. The official photographer, Fiona knew, would not come till five-thirty. Bill had already had a good look last week, and planned the best settings for his photographs.

The catering staff arrived, plus the parking attendants she'd hired to direct the guests' cars. Fiona kept moving and checking on things, whilst hoping and praying nothing would go wrong. Owen would kill her if it did.

At five, Kathryn went upstairs to get ready. She hadn't wanted to put her white silk suit on too early as she'd been afraid it might crush if she sat down.

Fiona didn't have to worry about that. Her dress didn't crush. Still, she had no intention of sitting down.

Bill arrived just on five-thirty, with his assistant and bevy of cameras. Fiona collected the bouquets from where they'd been resting in a cool spot in the pantry, and accompanied the photographer upstairs to collect the bride and bridesmaid for some pre-ceremony shots on the stairs.

Even Fiona had to admit that they both looked lovely. Corinne, especially. Like a fairy princess.

Bill didn't need her, so Fiona left him to it and went back downstairs to check that everything was ready for the ceremony and the reception afterwards. The sun was starting to set, throwing a spectacularly golden glow over the garden and the pool.

Everything was as ready as it was going to be. Fiona cast a final glance around the marquee, which looked superb with its elegantly draped ceiling and ultra-plush table settings. No expense had been spared, of course.

Fiona felt satisfied she'd done everything she could to make the wedding truly memorable, although there was a moment of panic when she realised the celebrant hadn't arrived. A quick call to his mobile reassured her he was on his way, in fact just around the corner.

Kathryn reappeared downstairs, looking truly lovely, but just a little strained. Weddings did that to the mothers. They did that to the consultants as well. Fiona told her she looked beautiful, pinned a delicate mauve orchid to her jacket—a red rose simply would not have done for this elegant lady—then helped her to another brandy.

'You have one too, Fiona,' she insisted.

Fiona didn't say no.

The first guests made an appearance around six-fifteen. Kathryn and Fiona both played hostess, directing everyone inside the huge front living rooms, where the pre-wedding drinks were being served and the orchestra was playing suitable music. Later on Fiona would move the musicians out onto the terrace.

'Doesn't everyone look lovely in their black and

white?' Kathryn whispered to Fiona at the door as the grandfather clock in the corner chimed six-thirty.

But Fiona wasn't listening to either Kathryn or the clock. Her ears had gone deaf as her attention focused on the car which had just purred to a stop at the front door.

A black Jaguar.

'I...I have to go check on the lights by the pool, Kathryn,' she said hurriedly, and left.

Oh, dear God, Fiona agonised as she fled through the house, her emotions in instant disarray, her control in danger of slipping. I thought I could do this but I can't! I just can't!

She moved as swiftly as her dress and high heels would allow, not stopping till she practically collided with one of the marble columns by the pool. Her hands shot out to grab at it, at first to steady herself, and then more tightly as a kind of impotent fury crashed through her. She wanted to crush the column between her hands, to topple it over, to dash it to the ground.

It took a great effort of will for Fiona to let the darned thing go. Slowly, she turned and leant her head back against the smooth marble, closing her eyes and taking a deep, deep breath.

Calm down, she ordered herself. What is this achieving? Where did you think you were running to? You have to see this through, Fiona. You have to drink from this cup.

A light tap on her shoulder sent her eyes flying open on a gasp.

'Goodness, Philip,' she exclaimed, struggling for composure. 'You...you startled me.'

'Sorry,' he said abruptly. 'You looked strange, standing there like that with your eyes shut. I thought you might be feeling unwell again. Not that you look sick,' he added in rueful tones. 'If I may say so, you look good enough to eat.'

Fiona gaped up at him and he slanted a travesty of a smile down at her.

'Not the sort of the thing the groom should be saying at this precise moment to a woman other than his bride?' he mocked. 'Perhaps not, but I can't seem to help the way you make me feel, Fiona. You seem to have a direct line to my male hormones.'

'Philip, I…I…'

'Yes, I know, you're sorry and I'm sorry,' he bit out. 'We're both sorry. Ahh…here's my best man, Steve, come to rescue me from myself. Don't worry,' he muttered under his breath. 'I haven't said anything and he won't recognise you.'

He didn't.

He'd changed a lot too, Fiona thought at first sight of the big sandy-haired man walking towards her. Better-looking and much more confident. But still not a patch on Philip.

He smiled as he looked her up and down. 'So this is the mysterious Fiona I never seem to meet. Philip didn't tell me you were a goddess when you weren't being a wedding consultant.'

'Fiona has a steady boyfriend—Mark,' Philip said drily. 'So save it.'

'Girls like Fiona always do, mate. But she's not wearing a ring, and all fair's in love and war. What are you doing after the wedding tonight, loveliness?'

Fiona might have been flattered by the jealousy on Philip's face—ten years ago. Now, she just felt sad.

'Sorry, Steve,' she responded politely. 'But Philip's right. There's another man in my life at the moment, and he's enough for me. Now I must go. You boys stay here and I'll see about getting the guests seated. No doubt Corinne will be a little late coming downstairs, Philip, but please...don't go away.'

'I'm not going anywhere, Fiona. I'm here to get married.'

'And I'm here to make sure you do.' She moved off, not looking back, even when Steve wolf-whistled at her departing figure.

Half an hour later Philip and Corinne were man and wife. Three hours later Corinne left the reception to go up and change into her going-away outfit, Carmel going with her to help. Philip started doing the rounds of thanking the guests for coming.

An increasingly depressed Fiona saw Steve making a beeline for her through the crowded marquee, so she fled into the house, where she found Kathryn standing at the bottom of the stairs, looking pale and shaken.

'Kathryn! What is it? Are you ill?'

The woman gave her a stricken look. 'Oh, Fiona, I've just had the most dreadful shock, and I...I don't know what to do!'

'What kind of a shock? Can I help?'

'I don't think anyone can help,' she said weakly.

'Let me be the judge of that,' Fiona said firmly. 'Now tell me what's happened.'

'It's Corinne,' the woman said reluctantly. 'I went upstairs to see if I could help in any way. I knocked on the door but there wasn't any answer. I...I opened the door, but the room seemed to be empty. I was puzzled and went in. It was then that I...that I...'

'That you what?' Fiona urged.

'Saw them,' Kathryn blurted out. 'In the bathroom...reflected in the mirror...'

marrying you. I thought it was an odd comment to make if she really loved you.'

'That's all?'

'That's all; I swear it. If you think I would deliberately let you marry Corinne, *knowing* the truth about her, then you can think again. I told you I cared about you, Philip, and I do.'

'Do you, now? In that case, then, lie for me in here. Tell Corinne you were the one who saw her with Carmel.'

Fiona's chin lifted. 'Gladly.'

Philip didn't knock. He just barged in. The bride and the bridesmaid were no longer in a compromising position—they were also fully dressed—but Philip's angry entry sent guilt leaping into their faces.

'Philip!' Corinne gasped. 'What is it? Is there anything wrong?'

'You tell me, Corinne. You tell me.'

The bride didn't look so beautiful with an ashen face and worried eyes. 'What…what do you mean?'

Carmel just looked terrified.

'Fiona came up to see if she could help you a little while ago,' Philip relayed harshly. 'She knocked, but you didn't answer, so she came in. It seems you and Carmel were…otherwise occupied,' he said mockingly. 'In the bathroom, I gather. That's right, isn't it, Fiona?'

'Yes,' she reaffirmed, and watched the two girls squirm.

'You have nothing to say, Corinne?' Philip ground out.

Guilt gradually changed to a sullen defiance. 'No,' came her sulky reply. 'There's not much point, is there, if she saw us?'

Philip looked at her bride with disgust. 'Just tell me one thing. When were you planning on leaving me? After our first baby was born, or earlier?'

'I had no intention of leaving you.'

Philip's face showed shock, and Corinne finally had the grace to look sorry.

'I did like you, Philip,' she insisted. 'Honestly. You're the only man I've ever met whom I could stand touching me. That's why it had to be you, don't you see?'

'I only see that you took my love and spat on it.'

'Oh, Philip, don't be so melodramatic. You never really loved me. I know because I know what it is to really love someone. I love Carmel and Carmel loves me. We've loved each other since we were fifteen. You liked me; that's all. I suited you. And I suited your mother. But you didn't love me.'

'You don't know what you're talking about,' he said coldly. 'Now I want you and your…girlfriend… out of this house. You have a car here, I presume?'

'Yes.'

'Then go downstairs, get in it, drive off and don't ever contact me again. You'll be hearing from me in due course. Not in person, however. I'll send the annulment papers to your father's address.'

'Don't tell him, Philip. I beg of you. He'll disinherit me. That's why I had to get married. Because he's paranoid about gays, and unmarried mothers, and just about everything else in this world.'

'I won't tell him. I won't tell anyone. Do you think I want to look that much a fool?'

'You're not a fool, Philip. You're a very nice man. You're—'

'Oh, for pity's sake, just go, will you?'

He watched over them like a vigilante till they did as he wanted. Only when their car had disappeared down the hill did he speak to Fiona, who'd stayed silently by his side all the time.

'Do you have a coat?' he asked abruptly.

'I have a jacket upstairs.'

'Get it and meet me here in two minutes. You'd better bring your handbag too, as well as anything else you might need. We're leaving.'

'Leaving!'

'You're just about to become my blushing bride. We're sneaking off early to avoid any of those 'just married' antics drunken wedding guests like to indulge in. My mother can tell Corinne's father his darling daughter and her beloved have departed prematurely.' Philip's smile was savagely sarcastic. 'He'll think she means the bride and groom. Then I'll have Steve grab a couple of selected people to run out and wave us off as we speed away in my Jag. They won't notice you're not a blonde through the tinted windows.'

'But—but...'

'Just think of the alternative, Fiona. Do you really want everyone to know this wedding turned out to be fiasco? What do you want people to remember it for? Its creativity and picture-perfect splendour? Or the fact the bride and groom never made it past the reception? Of course, I suppose I could always drive off with my mother, but I think she'd rather stay here.'

Fiona saw the sense of his idea, and sighed. 'I'll get my jacket.'

Philip's smile was chillingly hard. 'I thought you might.'

CHAPTER FOURTEEN

EVERYTHING went as Philip had planned, the Jaguar speeding off down the hill and through the open gates with no one at the wedding discovering the masquerade. The tyres squealed as Philip reefed the wheel to the right and sped up the road.

'Is there any need to go this fast?' Fiona complained.

'Yes,' he snapped, but he did slow down.

Fiona breathed a little easier, aware that Philip had to be very upset. What had just happened to him had been horrific. Whether he was deeply in love with Corinne or not was not the point. He cared for her and had committed himself to marrying her. He'd been expecting to go off on his honeymoon tonight with a beautiful girl who'd said she loved him and wanted to be his wife and the mother of his children.

Instead, he was driving into the night with a woman whom, any sexual attraction aside, he didn't particularly like anymore.

It was a drive to nowhere, for both of them.

'Where are you taking me?' Fiona asked tautly.

'Who cares?'

'I care.'

'Why? Because of your stupid bloody Mark? You don't love him,' he snarled.

'I never said I did.'

'Then why are you still sleeping with him?'

'I'm not.'

His head whipped round to stare at her.

'Watch the road,' she warned.

Philip was broodingly silent for a few seconds.

'When did you break up with him?' he asked.

'A while ago.'

'When?'

'I can't remember, exactly.'

He flashed her a scornful look. 'You don't care, do you, about any of us? We're all just male bodies to you, to be used and discarded at your pleasure and leisure.'

'That's not true. Not about you, anyway.'

'Oh, good. That makes me feel a whole lot better about this.'

Fiona sighed. 'Philip, I know you've been through a lot tonight. I'm truly sorry. If there was anything I could do to make you feel better, I'd do it.'

'Oh, there is, Fiona. Believe me. We're on our way there now so you can do it.'

'Pardon?'

'Don't play ignorant—or the innocent—with me. You know exactly where I'm taking you, and what we're going to do when we get there.'

'No,' she denied, her mind whirling. 'I don't.'

'In that case let me tell you. We're heading for the honeymoon suite I booked for tonight. It's just sitting there, waiting for me and my blushing bride, complete with harbour view, champagne, spa bath and satin sheets. You said you wanted to make me feel better, Fiona? Then be my blushing bride for tonight.'

Fiona's heart began to pound.

'No, I take that back,' Philip swept on caustically. 'I don't want a blushing bride. I want a female who knows exactly what she's doing and how to do it. In short, Fiona, I want you.'

'You don't mean that,' she said, shocked not only by his suggestion but by her immediate reaction to it.

A dark excitement began fizzing along her veins, tormenting her, tempting her.

'If you won't oblige me, honey, I'll find someone else who will. I won't have any trouble. I'll just cruise through some of the sleazier city bars and I'll soon find someone eminently qualified. She might even be pretty. Not that I'll care after I down a few Scotches. I nobly didn't drink much at my wedding dinner because I knew I'd have to drive, and I wanted to be right on the ball for my bride tonight. But the ball game has changed, hasn't it? Once I hand this chariot over to the hotel valet it's going to be full steam ahead in the alcohol department.'

'Philip, don't be insane! You can't go getting drunk and picking up some trampy female. You never know what diseases she might have, for one thing.'

'You're volunteering, then?'

Fiona didn't know what to do. She wanted to go with him. She couldn't deny it. Already, just thinking about being with him was turning her on.

But she also knew there was no future in it.

'You seem to be having some trouble making up your mind,' he drawled. 'What's your dilemma? Worried about catching something from *me*?'

'No…'

'It can't be pregnancy bothering you,' he ventured drily. 'A sophisticated, independent career girl like yourself would always have that base well covered.'

'I'm on the pill, yes,' she said stiffly. 'But I don't

usually tell my men-friends that. I always insist they use protection.'

'My, my, you *are* careful. Sorry, but I don't have any condoms with me. Contraception wasn't on my agenda for tonight. But I can stop at a chemist, if you like.'

'I haven't agreed to go with you yet.'

'Make up your mind, then,' he said, in a cold, hard voice. 'Once we get closer to the city it's hard to stop.'

Fiona tried to keep her cool in the face of the most appallingly corrupting thoughts.

'Fact is, Philip,' she said firmly, and tried to mean it, 'I don't go to bed with men who think I'm a slut. Or who treat me like one. Because I'm not! I'm not only discerning in my sexual partners, I demand respect from them.'

'I respect you.'

'No, you don't. You despise me for some reason. Frankly, I'm not sure why. If it's because I've been to bed with a few men for reasons other than love then you must despise yourself as well. I gathered from your mother that you haven't been in love once since we broke up—till Corinne came along, that is—yet I doubt you've been celibate all these years.'

He threw her a startled glance. 'Good grief, but you'd make a damned good defence lawyer! You have a definite skill in argument. And you *do* have a point, even if my mother could do with keeping her own counsel instead of telling a virtual stranger her son's private and personal business. Still, I stand corrected, and plead guilty to the crime of double standards. I will even apologise for any hasty judgements where you're concerned. Now will you spend the night with me?' And he flashed her a wickedly seductive smile.

Fiona felt herself wavering. 'I shouldn't,' she muttered. 'You'll probably regret it in the morning.'

He laughed. 'If you're worried that I might fall in love with you again, then don't be. I'm not a hormone-driven boy any longer. I know the difference between sex and love.'

Fiona winced. 'I just meant you might see things differently in the morning. You're acting on impulse tonight. And in anger.'

'Not entirely, Fiona,' he admitted drily. 'I've been thinking about having sex with you since I saw you leaning up against that pillar tonight. I married Corinne thinking about having sex with you. I promised to love, honour and cherish her while I was thinking how I'd like to lash you to that pillar, strip you naked, and keep you there for my pleasure for days on end.'

'Don't say things like that!' she gasped, her face flaming while her body burned with darkly answering desires.

'But it's true. That's what you do to me. You always did. You've no idea how much I used to want you, how nothing was ever enough, no matter how many times we did it, or how many ways.'

'Don't, Philip,' she choked out breathlessly.

'Yes, you're right. I have to shut up or I won't even make it to the bloody hotel. I'll pull over right here and now. And that's not what I want. Not at all. I want lots of room. I want you totally naked. And I want you more than once. The memory of you has tormented me for years, Noni,' he ground out. 'I won't be tormented tonight.'

She stared over at him and his angry face, his words echoing in her head. Masterful words. Erotic words. Exciting words.

He isn't himself, she reasoned. He's upset.

But then she thought…I don't care. I want him too, in whatever way he wants to have me. Because at least it will be Philip doing it to me, not some ghastly substitute. And when the sun comes up in the morning it will be Philip's face on the pillow beside me…

She looked over at him and caught his eye. 'How…how long till we're at the hotel?' she managed in strangled tones.

He smiled a slow, sexy, almost smug smile. They were on the same wavelength now, it said. Wanting the same things, driven by the same goals. 'Fifteen minutes, if we're lucky.'

'That's a long time.'

'You can wait, witch.'

'Maybe. Just.'

'This is going to be some night,' he muttered.

'Yes,' she agreed, and looked away from him. 'It is.'

The next fifteen minutes passed in a haze of desire the like of which Fiona had never known. It glazed her mind while it stirred her body, making the blood thrum through her veins and rush to her head till she felt dizzy and disorientated.

Perhaps she looked calm, sitting there, staring silently out at the city streets whizzing by, but she was anything but. Her head spun, and so did her thoughts. How could she do this to herself? How *could* she?

Because you *want* to, came the terrible truth.

You want to…

The Jag sped down the amazingly quiet Pacific Highway, and negotiated the Harbour Bridge with ridiculous ease. It was as though the fates were conspiring to hurry her to her doom, lest she change her mind and tell Philip to take her home. Or the devil himself making sure there was no other escape from the sexual tension which already had her in its tenacious grip; no escape but placing herself in Philip's impassioned hands once again.

Fiona feared that spending the night with Philip would break down the defences she'd built around her heart where falling in love with him again was concerned. By morning, she suspected, she wouldn't want just Philip's body but his heart as well.

But the Philip sitting beside her had a wounded heart, too wounded for anything remotely like falling in love with her in return. He wanted sex, not intimacy. Vengeance, not caring. He was being driven by lust, not love.

She was on a one-way ride to misery.

Ahh, but the wild excitement of that ride!

That was what was holding her in thrall, why she made no protest when the Jag screeched to a halt at one of Sydney's plushest inner-city hotels and Philip propelled her inside with almost indecent haste.

The honeymoon suite was on the top floor, a breathtakingly beautiful group of rooms decorated in pale blue and gold, with breathtakingly beautiful views of Sydney Harbour from every window.

Perversely, once Philip had her all to himself and the door was safely locked behind them, his sense of urgency seemed to dissipate. He walked slowly through the rooms, inspecting them for she knew not what. There seemed to be everything any honeymooner could possibly desire. A private balcony. An elegant sitting room. A cute little alcove set up for meals. A bedroom straight out of the Arabian Nights. A bathroom fit for a king, with a sunken circular spa bath, marble floors and benchtops, and the most exquisite gold taps.

'Philip,' she said at last when they'd returned to the sitting room. 'What are you doing?'

He looked up at her and smiled a wry smile. 'Calming down.'

'Oh...' Nothing was going to calm *her* down. Not inside, where her heart was racing madly and every nerve-ending she owned was on red alert

'Shall we take this into the bedroom?' he said, pointing to the bottle of champagne which was sitting in a silver ice bucket on the coffee table, along with a fresh fruit platter and two fluted crystal glasses.

'If you like,' she murmured, though all *she* wanted and needed in the bedroom was him. To use Corinne's favourite word, he looked utterly gorgeous, standing there in that beautiful black dinner suit.

Fiona couldn't wait to take it off him.

'You bring the glasses,' he told her, and scooped up the bucket.

Dropping her handbag by the table, she reefed off her jacket, picked up the glasses and hurried after him.

He opened the champagne and filled the glasses, before taking them from her hands and placing them on the bedside chest next to a very pretty gold lamp.

'What are you doing now?' she asked impatiently when Philip turned it on then walked round to turn on the matching lamp.

'Turn off the overhead light,' he ordered.

She did, and the room was immediately plunged into a romantic half-light, only the bed well lit, the blue satin quilt glowing under the golden circles of light from the lamps.

'Now, come over here.' He beckoned from where he was standing at the foot of the bed.

Her heart tripped. At last, he was going to make love to her. She felt self-conscious under the intensity of his gaze as she walked slowly towards him, and very aware of her own body: her breasts lushly full beneath her dress, her stomach tight in anticipation, her thighs trembling.

'Turn around,' he ordered when she was within an arm's distance.

She did.

She would have done anything he asked.

His fingertips brushed over her bare shoulders and she almost cried out.

She tensed even further as he took his time taking off her necklace, and then her earrings. 'I said I want you naked,' he murmured, his breath hot in her hair and over her neck.

'The…the zipper,' she told him shakily. 'It's at the back. Hidden.'

'Ahh, yes, I see.' She held her breath as he peeled it slowly down, her hands automatically clutching the dress up over her breasts when the back parted wide and threatened to fall.

'Let it go, Fiona,' he commanded.

She did, sucking in sharply when she was left standing there with nothing on but her pantyhose and high heels, a pool of white chiffon around her ankles.

'Step out of the dress carefully and walk over to the doorway,' he said in a low but firm voice. 'When you get there turn round, take off everything, then slip your shoes back on.'

Her pride screamed at her not to let him do this to her, reduce her to some kind of mindless sex object, to be displayed for his pleasure, positioned this way and that to satisfy whatever desire came into his mind.

But then she thought that maybe being a mindless sex object was safer. Maybe this way she wouldn't surrender her heart to him as well as her body. If she kept things to just sex, then she might survive this night with her self-esteem intact and her soul still her own.

So she did what he wanted, pricklingly aware of his gaze glued to her every step of the way, watching her strip naked for him, then slide her feet back into her high heels to stand there like some call girl.

'No, stay there a minute,' he rasped when she went to walk back towards him. 'I want to just look at you while I undress.' And he yanked his bow tie undone.

Fiona watched him watch her while *he* stripped. She wasn't sure which excited her the most, seeing his body slowly unfolding, or displaying her own nudity so shamelessly.

He was more beautiful than she remembered. And more awesome.

'Now you can come here,' he said, after he'd tossed all their clothes aside and sat down on the end of the bed.

She almost couldn't obey him, her legs suddenly like jelly. She forced them to move and finally made her way shakily towards him. Once she got there he directed her to straddle his thighs but to stay standing.

By this point she was beyond denying him anything, and in truth she found the position dizzyingly exciting, with her legs wide apart, his hands gripping her thighs and his mouth on a level with her fluttering stomach, so close she could feel the heat of his breath in her navel.

His hands released their firm grip to run with tantalising slowness over her body, starting at the back of her knees. Up her legs they travelled, taking their time on her taut buttocks before finding the small of her back. Once there, he trickled his fingertips around her waist, skimmed up over her ribs, then briefly over the tips of her breasts, before trailing back down across her tensing stomach.

Fiona sucked in a sharp breath as he drew close to the curls at the apex of her thighs. But he bypassed that area and finally returned to her knees, touching her everywhere but where she desperately wanted to be touched. By the time he'd repeated this torture several times, her stomach was like a rock, and her nipples like nails.

But, inside, she was a melting, quivering mess.

When his hands finally slipped between her legs her gravelly moan told of the intensity of her arousal and frustration. When his thumbs brushed against the bursting bud of flesh which was burning in erotic anticipation for any kind of touch at all, she gasped, and her knees began to go.

'Don't move,' he commanded sharply, and she really tried not to. But when he started further serious exploration of everything which made her a woman, she wanted to scream and writhe and beg him to stop. She bit her bottom lip and willed herself to be silent and still. But it was becoming unbearable. She was going to come. She had to. She…

He stopped, and a tormented sob broke from her lips.

Philip made a similar sound as he grabbed hold of her already wobbly knees and yanked them down onto the bed on either side of him, the tip of his stunning erection perfectly positioned to probe at the heated heart of her. Fiona could not wait a moment longer, sinking down onto him with a long, low moan of pleasure. When she also presented one of her aching nipples to his lips, he willingly obliged, suckling on it like a starving infant.

Wrapping her arms around his head, she began to ride him, feeling all primal woman with her man both at her breast and deep inside her body, his exquisitely swollen flesh stroking her insides as she rocked up and down.

She'd hardly started when she came with a rush, gasping as the spasms hit. Philip groaned and bit down on her nipple, grabbing her hips and urging her to continue moving all through her orgasm, and further.

Fiona was astonished to find the pleasure not draining away as it usually did when she climaxed. The rapture rolled onto another level, where the sensations became even more addictive and electric. When Philip finally exploded within her, she came again. Violently.

Afterwards, they collapsed together back onto the bed, Philip clasping her to him, muttering something into her hair which she could not make out.

For ages she lay sprawled across him, feeling dazed and disorientated. She could not remember ever having come twice like that, even back in the old days.

Of course, Philip was an even more skilled lover now. She could see that. And maybe she was a little more needy. In the last decade no man had ever really fulfilled her in a sexual sense. She'd held herself much too distant from them emotionally to really let go in the bedroom. Only with Philip did she feel this abandon, this total lack of pretence.

Which was why he was so dangerous to her.

Suddenly he opened his eyes, and smiled up at her. 'Recovered yet?' he said, before abruptly rolling over and scooping her under him. 'God, but you're so incredibly sexy,' he muttered, stroking her hair out of her face and planting a kiss on her mouth. 'I could just eat you up. But not right now. Right now I'm going to go run us a spa bath. And fix us up with some refreshment. I'd forgotten how making love to a goddess took it out of a guy. Now don't go away!' he commanded as he withdrew and clambered off the bed.

Fiona's glazed eyes followed him lustfully. She was beyond going anywhere. She was beyond anything except blind obedience to his will.

'I feel very decadent,' she murmured ten minutes later, leaning back against the bath, sipping champagne and eating a strawberry from the fruit platter Philip had brought in from the sitting room.

He grinned from his position opposite her.

'You *look* very decadent,' he said, his eyes raking over her breasts which were just on show above the bubbles.

She didn't blush. She was way beyond blushing too.

'How's your murder case going?' she asked, and he shot her a disbelieving look.

'You want to talk about my work? *Now?*'

'Just curious. What happened?'

'We won. The jury acquitted her.'

'I knew you would,' she said, and his eyebrows arched.

'Such confidence! To what do I owe that?'

She sipped some more champagne. 'To my having faith in your abilities. And your passion.'

'My *passion*? What do you mean by that?'

'You are the only man I've met who feels things as strongly as you do. You don't let anything or anyone sway you from doing what you want to do.'

'You could be right. But I'm not sure if that's a good thing or a bad thing.'

'It can't be a *bad* thing.'

'That depends. But let's not get serious. I haven't come here tonight to be serious. Drink up.' He slid over and topped up her glass, then slid back again. 'I want you nice and tipsy by the time we get out of this bath.'

'Why's that?'

'I seem to recall you're wonderfully willing to please when you're tipsy.'

Fiona drank up, telling herself that getting drunk was good. Drunk was unthinking and uncaring. Drunk had nothing to with depth and everything to do with superficiality.

'Fill 'er up again,' she said, and held out the empty glass for restocking. To be honest, she was already on the way to a nicely intoxicated state. She hadn't eaten much all night, and was probably a bit dehydrated as well. The champagne was certainly hitting her blood-stream hard, making her light-headed and just a tad reckless.

Which was a pretty funny thought. How much more reckless could she get? A giggle escaped, and Philip frowned at her.

'I want you tipsy,' he warned, 'not paralytic.'

'I'm a long way from being paralytic, Philip. Trust me.'

'That's usually the man's line.'

'If you want me to stop, then just say so,' she said. 'I'm yours to command tonight.'

'Only tonight?'

Her eyes danced at him over the rim of the glass. 'Let's take one night at a time, shall we?'

'In that case, I think it's time we got *this* night on the road again, don't you?'

Getting out the sunken spa bath and getting dry was a true test of Fiona's level of intoxication. Not nearly drunk enough, she decided when Philip took one the huge fluffy blue towels and gently dried every inch of her.

His unexpected tenderness started things happening inside her which were worryingly emotional as opposed to strictly sexual. Her heart contracted when he told her how beautiful she was—*and* when he stroked the towel softly down her back, kissing her spine from top to bottom. By the time he handed her the towel and asked her to reciprocate she was in a state of turmoil.

She simply *had* to change things back to just sex.

The trouble was, the moment she sank boldly to her knees in front of him, she was overcome with such feeling for him, such…caring…that she lost the plot. Before she knew it she was making love to him with her mouth and her hands with a passion and a commitment that could only come from a woman in love. She prayed for him to stop her, but he didn't, and in the end she couldn't.

Afterwards, he gave her another glass of champagne and looked at her with thoughtful eyes.

'You always were good at that,' he murmured. 'But you're even better now.'

'So are you,' she returned, desperate to cling to the illusion that it was still only lust directing her actions.

'Is that a compliment, or a request? No matter,' he

laughed, and scooped her up into his arms. 'Either will get you what you want,' he said, and carried her back to bed.

She tried to hold herself distant from him. But how could she when he started kissing her all over again with such thoroughness? Her mouth, her neck, her breasts, her stomach. By the time he moved beyond her stomach she moaned her total surrender and let her legs fall wantonly apart.

He started doing what he'd done on his father's dining room table, his large strong hands holding her firmly captive so that she was powerless to twist away from the devastating forays of his wickedly knowing tongue. It tormented her for ages, flicking lightly over electrified nerve-endings before sliding slowly inside, then all too swiftly withdrawing to start the teasing process all over again. When she actually began to beg, he lifted her bottom higher and drove his tongue deep, finding a spot which brought a scream to her throat.

Her back arched violently from the bed, then stayed that way as she came and came and came.

Finally, the terrifyingly endless contractions did end, and he let her go.

With a death-rattling sigh, her spine gradually un-kinked and sank back down onto the bed, her arms flopping wide. Her eyelids felt so heavy she was sure any second she would fall asleep.

Philip sat up between her leaden thighs, his eyes glittering with dark triumph as he stared down at her spreadeagled body. 'I love you like this,' he muttered. 'You haven't the energy to stop me doing whatever I want.' Leaning forward, he slid his hands under her bottom again, and eased her forward, up onto his lap and onto him.

Her groan of protest was laughingly ignored.

'See what I mean?' he mocked, his hands reaching down to play with her breasts. He plucked at their still erect nipples and she groaned in protest again, this time not at all convincingly.

His eyes flashed almost angrily at the sound.

'Time to tell you the score, my sweetly insatiable Fiona,' he growled as he began to move slowly within her. 'First, you're not going to have any other men-friends from now on except me. I'm going to be your only lover. Yes, the one and only,' he repeated as his rhythm quickened. 'You'll come out with me when I want you to; stay the night with me when I want you to; *do* what I want you to. Do I make myself clear?'

Fiona wanted to tell him to go to hell. But she could not seem to find the words, or the will. Oh, she was weak where he was concerned! Horribly, horribly weak.

'Do…I…make…myself…clear?' he repeated, his thrusting becoming almost manic, his face contorting.

'Yes,' she cried out as her body began to betray her one more time. 'Yes!'

You've made yourself very clear.

Very, very clear.

CHAPTER FIFTEEN

FIONA found some character in the morning, as well as a strong surge of anger. Mostly directed at herself. How *could* she have let Philip treat her so disgracefully, as if she was some kind of sex toy!

It was immaterial that she'd woken feeling physically fantastic, with clear eyes, glowing skin and not a trace of a hangover. Sexual ecstasy was no excuse for the disgusting way she'd behaved!

As for falling in love with Philip again...

That was her most unforgivable sin of all!

She would not entertain the thought of it. Neither would she put up with that ridiculous love-slave relationship Philip had made her agree to when she'd been incapable of thinking straight, let alone telling him where he could stick his typically male ego-driven demands.

The man must be insane to think that any intelligent, independent woman would put up with such a masochistic and one-sided relationship! She hadn't become the person she was today to revert to the sort of behaviour that that silly ninny named Noni had indulged in! Good grief. The very idea!

Once Fiona was showered and dressed, with her hair brushed, her jacket on and two good strong cups of coffee inside her, she carried a cup into a still sleeping Philip and sat down on the bed.

Her eyes were firm when they moved to Philip, but the moment she made eye contact with his sleeping form Fiona wavered again. Oh, God. He looked so beautiful and sexy lying there, with his long eyelashes resting on his tanned cheek and his lovely mouth softly parted in sleep. She groaned as her gaze travelled slowly over his naked body—what there was of it on display, that was—and she thought of the intense pleasure that body could bring her.

Was she prepared to risk losing that pleasure for the sake of pride?

Her spine straightened, her chin lifting proudly. Yes, she told herself. Her answer had to be yes!

Of course, it was incredibly easy to come to that valiant resolve with Philip unconscious. A bit like walking into a lion's cage when the lion was drugged, or dead, then bragging afterwards of one's bravery.

Not much of a challenge, that.

What if, when she awakened Philip, he grabbed her and dragged her into bed with him? What if he wouldn't take her no for an answer and proceeded to coerce and corrupt her with more fantastic sex till she begged him to use her any way he wanted, as often as he wanted?

The possibility appalled her.

Jumping up from the bed, she swiftly plonked the dangerously rattling cup and saucer on the bedside table and was about to flee when Philip stirred, yawned and rolled over, the blue satin sheet shifting to a level around his hips just short of indecent.

Before Fiona could do more than blink, two beautiful blue eyes popped open and looked straight up into hers.

They flicked over her, frowning.

Their owner immediately sat bolt-upright, the sheet slipping down to his thighs.

'Fiona?'

'Yes?' she choked out, feeling decidedly flustered as she forcibly dragged her eyes back up to his face.

He glanced at his watch and frowned some more. 'It's seven in the morning. Why are you up and dressed?'

Fiona pulled herself together. 'It's Monday. I have to go home and change, then go to work.'

'But I'm on holiday for the next week. I was hoping you might have some time off and spend it with me.'

Oh, God, she thought. A whole week of the same as last night. Seven days and seven nights.

'Then you thought wrong, Philip,' she said coolly, even while her face felt hot.

'But you're your own boss, aren't you?'

'Yes,' she said meaningfully. 'I am.'

He ignored that one. 'Is this for me?' he asked, picking up the coffee cup.

'Yes.'

'Thanks.' He took a couple of sips. 'It's perfect,' he complimented warmly. 'Just the way I like it.'

'I know.'

He smiled up at her. 'You know everything I like, don't you?'

She wanted to slap his beautifully arrogant face.

'Philip,' she said sternly.

'Yes, darling?'

Oh, that was low, she thought mutinously. And downright sarcastic.

'We have to talk about last night.'

'What about it?'

'What I agreed to...'

'Yes?'

'I misled you, I'm afraid.'

The cup stilled halfway to his mouth. He lowered

it very, very slowly and gave her a long, terrifyingly hard look. 'In what way?' he finally asked.

She swallowed. 'The thing is, Philip, I want more from a relationship than just sex.'

His eyebrows shot upwards, as though she'd genuinely surprised him. 'Really?'

'Yes, really. I won't play sex-slave for any man, not even you.'

'You did a pretty good job last night.'

'I indulged you, because I knew you were hurting.'

'*Indulged* me?'

'Yes.'

He laughed. 'You indulged *yourself*, Fiona. You loved every minute of it.'

Fiona could not deny he'd given her great pleasure.

'I know exactly what you want from a relationship with a man, sweetheart,' he went on, his tone mocking and cynical. 'And that's what I gave you last night. I'm also well aware your men-friends have a use-by date, but I wouldn't have thought mine had run out just yet. I gather from Owen your lovers last a little longer than one night.'

Fiona was truly taken aback. Owen? What had Owen been telling Philip about her and her lovers?

She might have said something, but was distracted by Philip throwing back the sheet and climbing from the bed.

'I can see, however,' he stated as he strutted towards her, stark naked, 'that you *do* have your priorities. Work still comes first, if you'll pardon the pun. So!' He chucked her under the chin, shutting her startled mouth in time for a swift peck on the lips. 'How about after work tonight? We could go out to dinner somewhere. Then you can have me for afters,' he added, with the sort of smile which would have seduced a nun.

She would have had him then and there, if she hadn't been so spitting mad!

'What did Owen say to you about me?' she persisted heatedly.

'Nothing but the truth, so don't go getting all hot under the collar. Look, it suits me very well that you don't want to get married or have children. I've given up on both those fronts. Frankly, I don't seem to be too lucky in the love and marriage arena.'

Fiona didn't know whether to scream, or to cry. She felt simultaneously angry and despairing.

'For pity's sake, don't make a fuss when you get to work,' Philip said wearily. 'Poor Owen only thought he was doing the right thing, warning me of your love 'em and leave 'em nature. He couldn't possibly have anticipated that what you offer a man is exactly what I'm looking for at this moment, to get over Corinne. So calm down and stop acting like a self-righteous little hypocrite.'

Fiona found some comfort in fury. '*You* ought to talk,' she snapped. 'You told me you didn't fancy me. You said I was too skinny, for one thing.'

'I lied.'

She just stared at him, and he shrugged.

'The truth is I've been lying ever since you walked into my life again. I should never have gone through with that sham of a marriage to Corinne. She was right when she said I didn't truly love her. How could I have, when all I could think of was you?'

Fiona stared up at him, hope bursting into flower in her heart. What was he saying? That he was in love with *her*? It didn't seem possible, but surely this couldn't be just lust looking back down at her with such hot passion in his eyes. Surely not.

Her heart lurched, then flipped right over. 'Philip,' she groaned aloud, and those blazing blue eyes suddenly went cold.

'You don't have to worry, darling,' he said with a sardonic smile, crushing that flower of hope as surely as if he'd slipped it under his foot and stomped on it. 'I'm not about to declare my undying devotion. I'm merely stating that a man truly in love with one woman doesn't spend all his waking hours wanting to have sex with another. And believe me, I've wanted to have sex with you these past ten weeks like there was no tomorrow. Old flames perhaps. But damned stubborn ones. From your responses last night, I suspect you've been suffering from the same old smoulder. But we're on the way to a cure now, aren't we? In six months or so, with a bit of luck, we'll have burnt out the fires once and for all. Meanwhile, at least I'll be able to get a good night's sleep. So, what time do you want me to pick you up tonight?'

Fiona could barely function under the weight of her despair. 'What?'

'Tonight. Do you want me to pick you up from work or at your place? I thought I'd go spend the day with my mother, since I haven't anything else to do, and I think the old dear might be wanting some company after last night's fiasco.'

'But…but I have to come out there this afternoon myself,' she protested. 'I have to see that everything has been cleared away properly.'

'Perfect. I'll see you out there, then.'

Fiona could think of nothing worse! 'But…but…'

'Fiona, darling, what is it?' he said, taking her into

his arms and giving her an almost concerned look. 'Have I upset you in some way? Look, of course there'll be more to our relationship than just sex. We'll go out together. We'll spend time together. We'll even talk sometimes. We just won't make plans for a future together. There's no point, is there?'

'I…I guess not.' Not unless he loved her.

'Good. We've got that settled, then.'

'But…'

'Now what time will you be at Kenthurst?'

'Around two.'

'Two it is, then.'

'But what about your mother?' she finally managed to blurt out.

'What about her?'

'I don't want her to know about…about *us*!'

'Why not?'

'Because…because I like her and she likes me and I…I wouldn't want her to look at me like she's ashamed of me or something.'

Philip just stared at her. 'You mean you *care* about what she thinks of you?'

'Yes. Yes, I do.'

'I see. Surprising. Well, all right, I won't tell her about us. I probably wasn't going to, anyway. I'll see you around two, then.' And, with a parting peck, he turned and walked into the bathroom.

CHAPTER SIXTEEN

'How dare you say such things to Philip about me?' Fiona ranted and raved to Owen as she thumped his desk with angry fists. 'You had no right. It was unforgivable. In fact, I will *never* forgive you!'

Oh-oh, Owen thought sheepishly. She's found out I gave Philip a résumé of her recent love life.

But how? he puzzled. Why? *When?*

She certainly hadn't known anything last evening, when he'd spoken to her on her mobile, halfway through the reception.

She'd sounded very calm, if a little subdued, as she'd told him that the ceremony had gone off very well and the reception was proceeding smoothly. What on earth had happened between Fiona and the groom after that?

Still, given the intensity of her rage, Owen thought it wise to try the low-level approach of enquiry. 'Er... I'm not sure I know what you're referring to, Fiona,' he tried.

'Oh, yes, you do, you selfish, conniving, manipulative bastard! You were worried something might spring up again between Philip and myself and spoil your chance to have your name on a fancy society wedding, so you told him I was some kind of good-time girl who slept around and had absolutely no interest in marriage and children.'

'I never said you slept around!' Owen protested. 'I merely pointed out that your admirers didn't have a good track record of going the long haul with you. As for your attitude to marriage and children, you hardly made that a secret, Fiona.'

'You have no idea what you've done!' she wailed.

'No. I have to admit I don't. What does it really matter what I said, now that the groom is safely married and off on his honeymoon? You'll never see him again.'

There was something about the way she groaned which alarmed Owen.

'What is there here that I don't know?' he said worriedly.

When Fiona slumped in a chair in front of his desk and buried her face in her hands, Owen began to panic.

'Fiona! I demand you tell me what's going on!'

Fiona's face burst out of her hands and she looked quite manic, with her brown eyes very big in her pale face. 'You want to know what's going on? I'll tell you what's going on—although what's *gone* on is infinitely more titillating!'

Titillating?

Owen didn't know whether to be intrigued or unnerved.

Fiona jumped to her feet again and began to pace agitatedly around the room. 'Where shall I start?' She tossed the words with patently false flippancy. 'The moment the mother of the groom discovered that her new daughter-in-law was in love with the bridesmaid, and not her son?'

Owen gaped.

'Or should I go back to Philip's first wedding day? To me! The day I lost his baby, then gave him up because I was told I wasn't good enough for him and I couldn't bear the thought that he would one day look at me and hate me, even though I loved him more than life itself!'

Now Owen grimaced, his sympathetic heart squeezing tight. Oh, the poor darling…

'No, that sounds far too melodramatic,' Fiona swept on. 'Not to mention dead and gone. So I shall move on to Philip asking me to pretend to be Corinne last night, after Corinne and Carmel drove off together. Just to fool the guests, mind. He didn't want anyone to know that his bride preferred the bridesmaid to him. Which was understandable, I thought, and why I agreed. As well as to protect our wonderful business, of course!' she threw at Owen with a savage glance.

'Good thinking,' Owen praised, trying to make light in the face of whatever coming disaster Fiona was about to recount.

'Only *then* darling Philip wanted me to pretend to be Corinne in a more personal way, didn't he? And I—silly, weak fool that I am—couldn't say no. So we spent the night together and now I've fallen in love with him again, only this time he doesn't love me at all! He thinks I'm just good for sex and he can use me till he gets over his broken heart, or bruised ego, or whatever he's feeling at the moment. And what really kills me, Owen, what I just can't handle in the cold light of day, is that I'm going to *let* him!'

With that, Fiona's face crumpled and she burst into tears. Owen leapt to his feet and raced around to lead her over to the cosy two-seater which he kept for visiting brides and grooms. Fiona fell into it, still weeping. Owen perched on the coffee table in front of it and patted her knees.

'There, there,' he said soothingly. 'Cry it out. You can probably do with a good cry. You don't cry enough for a female. And when you're finished, I'm going to tell you how it *really* is.'

Fiona didn't quite take in Owen's words for a minute or two as she blubbered uncontrollably. But gradually his last remark *did* sink in and her tear-stained face slowly lifted. She took the spotted handkerchief Owen was holding out to her and wiped her nose, then frowned up at him.

'What do you mean? How it *really* is?'

'Why do you think I told Philip what I did?' He explained. 'Because he was showing signs of *real* feelings towards you. And I'm not talking about sexual feelings. I'm talking deep emotional involvement, here. Believe me, I've been around enough couples in love to see the signs.'

Fiona's whole insides tightened as she tried not to hope too much. 'You...you think Philip's in love with me?' she asked.

'Let's just say I think he's still emotionally involved with you.'

'Why didn't you *say* something?' she burst out.

'Hell, Fiona, why would I? I thought you felt Philip was as much an unwanted complication in your life as *I* did. The man was marrying someone else, for pity's sake. It wasn't my place to open my big bib and claim he hadn't gotten over you.'

'Are you sure about this, Owen? I mean...are you *sure* he still cares about me?' She didn't dare use the word 'love.' If she started believing Philip loved her, only to find out he didn't, she would surely go mad!

Owen took her hands in his. 'How can I be absolutely sure?' he said. 'He's never actually said anything to me. I'm going on instinct. But you're the one who spent the night with the man. If he loves you, there must have been some moments when he told you of that love. Maybe not in so many words, but in his actions.'

Fiona wished that had been the case. Oh, yes, he'd been tender a couple of times. Tender and gentle and complimentary. But he'd also been cynical and kinky, and even cruel at other times. Would a man in love deliberately get his beloved drunk, so he could have his wicked way with her?

'I don't think it's love he feels for me,' she said unhappily.

'Why don't you ask him?' Owen suggested.

Fiona's eyes blinked wide.

'And, while you're at it, why don't you tell him you love him? And then tell him the truth about why you left him all those years ago. I'll bet you never have.'

'I... I...'

'Time for the truth, dear friend,' Owen said firmly. 'You'll never have a better chance, or a better reason.'

The truth...

Yes, she realised, even while the thought of exposing her soul brought nausea to her throat. Owen was right.

It was time for the truth, the whole truth and nothing but the truth!

So help me God, she prayed.

CHAPTER SEVENTEEN

FIONA sat in her car by the side of the road outside the gates of Kathryn's house, and watched the toing and froing of trucks as the marquee and everything which had been shipped in for the wedding was removed.

She felt sick with nerves. And sick with hope.

If only Owen was right...

But even if he was, that didn't mean everything would turn out all right. Because Philip might not believe *her* about why she'd left him ten years ago, and about what she felt for him now. His opinion of her present-day character was awfully low.

Still, she *had* to try. Owen was right. She'd never have a better chance. If she left it, things would only get more complicated, and more confusing.

Gathering her courage, she turned on the engine, then drove in through the open gates and on up to the house. It was just on noon.

High Noon, she thought, her stomach churning.

The front door was wide open and a team of carpet cleaners were still busy, putting the living room carpets back in order after some inevitable spills and stains. Fiona had arranged for them to come in the morning after the wedding, as she'd arranged everything else.

She made her way through the house and finally found Kathryn and Philip sitting together at a table on the thankfully empty and restored back terrace. There

175

were no workmen or cleaners hovering around to disturb or overhear what Fiona had to say.

Philip rose from his seat on seeing her, his expression surprised, whispering, 'You're early,' as he held out a seat for her.

Kathryn, who was looking tired, gave her a wan smile. 'I'm glad you're here, Fiona,' she said. 'I wanted to thank you for what you did for Philip last night.'

Fiona's eyes met Philip's wry ones.

No sign of love there, she thought unhappily.

'It saved everyone a lot of embarrassment,' Kathryn went on. 'You know, I still can't get over Corinne's abysmal behaviour. I have no problem with gay people, but what she did was quite wicked—pretending to love Philip and tricking him into marrying her just so she could have a legitimate child. I'm truly amazed you've taken it as well as you have, Philip.'

'Fiona made me realise I had a lucky escape,' he returned drily. 'I might not have found out till after it was too late.'

'I shudder to think about it!' his mother exclaimed.

'Speaking of finding out things,' Fiona began, before her courage failed her.

Philip flashed her a puzzled glance, but Fiona didn't look at him, knowing in her heart that it was now or never.

'I have something to say to you, Kathryn, which Philip knows about but which we've kept from you.'

'*Fiona,*' Philip warned sharply.

'No, Philip. I've decided I want your mother to know.'

'Know what?' Kathryn looked bewildered.

Fiona gave her a pleading smile. 'Please don't be

angry with me, Kathryn. I...I really didn't mean any harm. I can see now, however, that it was wrong of me not to tell you the truth up front, and I regret it sincerely.'

'The truth? What truth?'

'About my true identity.' Fiona swallowed, then plunged on. 'You see, ten years ago people didn't know me as Fiona Kirby. Back then I was called Noni Stillman.'

Kathryn gasped while Philip groaned.

'For pity's sake, Fiona,' he ground out. 'Did you have to blurt it out like that?'

She turned surprisingly steady eyes his way. 'There *was* no easy way, Philip. The truth, I'm beginning to understand, is never easy.'

Kathryn's colour gradually came back to normal and her eyes washed disbelievingly over Fiona. 'I would *never* have recognised you.'

'Yes, I know.'

'You've changed so much!'

'Yes, she has,' Philip bit out, and his mother twisted round to frown at her son.

'But *you* recognised her?'

'Of course,' he said drily.

'Yes,' she murmured, nodding. 'Yes, of course. Yes, I see.'

Her gaze swung back to Fiona, who was astonished to see the woman's eyes fill with tears. And something else.

'I *do* see,' Kathryn told her softly, and Fiona suddenly recognised what that 'something else' was.

Sympathy, and understanding.

Emotion crashed through Fiona. Kathryn *knew*. She didn't have to explain a word to her. Not a single word. Philip was the one who didn't see, or understand. He was blind to her reasons for doing this. He just sat there, his face tight with fury and frustration that Fiona had chosen to go over his head and tell his mother who she was.

'Happy now?' he snapped. 'Maybe you'd like to confess all, while you're at it. Maybe you'd like to tell my mother where we spent last night and what we did most of the night.'

When Fiona looked crushed, an amazingly unshocked Kathryn turned to her son again and just shook her head at him. 'Oh, Philip, don't,' she reproached. 'You don't know what you're doing to her.'

'What *I'm* doing to *her*?' He exploded onto his feet. 'What about what *she's* done to *me*? What she did ten years ago? What she's been doing ever since she showed up in my life again? I've been in hell, I tell you. She's the devil in disguise, pretending to be sweet and nice when all the while she takes men's souls and destroys them. Well, she's not going to destroy me a second time. This time it's *her* who's going to be destroyed. You liked last night, Fiona?' he jeered nastily. 'Well, savour the memories, honey, because it was our swansong. I won't be seeing you again. Or touching you again. *Ever!*'

Kathryn was gaping up at him while Fiona desperately tried to cling on to the slim hope that the hatred blazing down at her was not really hatred but the other side of love.

She rose shakily to her feet and looked him straight in the eye. 'But I love you, Philip,' she said bravely. 'And I loved you ten years ago.'

'You're a damned liar! You didn't love me ten years ago. You told me you didn't. And you *showed* me you didn't. You left me, without a backward glance. Was that the action of someone in love?'

'Yes!' Kathryn pronounced, and stood up as well.

Fiona stared at her. And so did Philip.

'Sit down, the pair of you!' she ordered.

Startled, they did.

Kathryn sat down last, leaning over briefly to pat Fiona's nearest arm before turning her attention to her son.

'I never said anything to you about this before, Philip, because I didn't see any point. On top of that, I didn't *know* anything of this till just before your father died. But the situation's changed now. Noni—I mean Fiona—has come back into your life and you *have* to know the truth about what happened that night ten years ago.'

Bewilderment held Fiona silent as Kathryn gave her a warmly apologetic glance.

'This sweet child didn't want to leave you. She loved you very, very much. But losing the baby had upset and depressed her a great deal, making her very susceptible to suggestion. When you were out of the house, your father took deliberate advantage of her emotional state to talk her into giving you up. For *your* sake, he insisted. And for her own, he pretended.'

'No, just *listen*!' Kathryn insisted when Philip went to open his mouth. 'He told her you were too immature to know your own mind, that you'd fancied yourself in love many times before and that it was a common flaw in young men to confuse sex and love. He told her that one day you'd wake up and realise you weren't in love with her, and then you'd hate her for trapping you into an unsuitable marriage. He played on her own vulnerability and insecurities, making her think she wasn't good enough for you, that she'd drag you down and make you unhappy. And in this I bear a great amount of blame. I was very unkind in my criticism of you back then, Fiona. I didn't realise till after you'd long gone how mean and snobbish I was. I've always wanted the opportunity to say how sorry I am.'

'It's all right, Kathryn,' Fiona mumbled.

'No, it's *not* all right. What I did was very wrong. And what your father did, Philip, was very wrong too. And he knew it. It played on his conscience at the end, which is why he confessed his unhappy part in all this to me.'

'It didn't take him long to convince her, though, did it?' Philip said sharply. 'I was only gone half an hour.'

'You know what a clever talker he was. A brilliant negotiator. He could make black seem white once he got going. Still, he had a great weapon to use. Fiona's love for you. He made her believe she was doing the right thing, giving you up.'

'But *why*?' Philip cried, clearly anguished by this amazing revelation. 'Why would he do such a thing? He *knew* how much I loved her. He *knew*!'

'Oh, Philip, he was your father, and he wanted so much for you. *Too* much. He thought he was being cruel to be kind. He thought *he* was doing the right thing too.'

'The right thing!' Philip groaned. 'Oh, God, if only he'd known what he put me through.'

'He put Fiona through a lot as well, son,' Kathryn reminded him gently.

Fiona watched, dry-mouthed, as Philip's shocked eyes turned back to hers.

'Is this true, what my mother's saying?' he asked her. 'Is that the way it really happened?'

Fiona was in shock herself. She hadn't realised how devious Philip's father had been. She'd thought he was being kind and gentle with her that night, when all the while he'd…he'd…

Tears pricked her eyes as the reality of the man's perfidy struck home.

'Yes,' she choked out.

Philip's face struggled for composure. 'Why didn't you tell me all this when we met up again?'

'How could I when you were marrying someone else?'

'Yes, just nine years after *you* did,' he said accusingly.

Fiona dashed away the threatening tears and tried to remain strong. 'I should never have married Kevin. I admit it. I didn't love him. But I was lonely and he was nice to me. At the time I needed…someone… something. I was very wrong to marry him. As soon as I realised that I set him free, and then set about relying on myself alone in the future. I didn't want to hurt anyone else. And, yes, I didn't want to be hurt myself. I grew hard. I can see that now. Hard and tough. And I *did* hurt people. Men who liked me. Maybe some of them even loved me. I'm not proud of that. When we met up again, I truly believed I was over you. Fiona was nothing like Noni, I told myself. She didn't fall helplessly in love, certainly not with the same man.'

Fiona stiffened her spine for the ultimate confession. 'But I *have* fallen helplessly in love with you again, Philip, and there's nothing I can do about it. I'm yours…if you want me.'

He was speechless. But his eyes spoke volumes. Emotion melted their earlier hardness and love washed over her in warm, wonderful waves.

Kathryn cleared her throat and stood up. 'I think it's time I went to see about the carpet cleaners.'

'It…it never occurred to me that you might have given me up for love,' he said thickly.

'Believe me, I regretted it later.'

'I never forgot you,' he told her, and reached for her hands across the table.

She took them, and her heart almost burst with happiness. 'Nor I you.'

Their fingers entwined.

'I used to go into every fish and chip shop I saw, thinking you might be there, behind the counter.'

'I used to ring your phone number, just so I could hear your voice.'

'I hated thinking of you with someone else's child.'

'I would never have *had* anyone else's child. I only ever wanted yours, Philip,' she said, and squeezed his hands even more tightly.

'Will you try to have my child again, Fiona?'

'If you want me to.'

'If I want you to. My God, do you know how much I love you?'

Her smile was soft and warm. 'You can tell me if you like.'

His mouth twisted wryly. 'All I can think of are clichés, like how wide is the ocean, and how deep is the sea?'

Her smile widened. 'They'll do for now. I'll let you show me in person later.'

'You're a wicked woman.'

'If I am, then you're entirely responsible. Till I met

you, I didn't even *like* sex. I thought it was highly overrated and very icky.'

He smiled. 'I see you've gotten over your revulsion.'

'Philip,' she said, and he shot her a worried look.

'What?'

'I have only one thing to ask.'

'Anything.'

'Promise me you won't ask me to marry you?'

'Why ever not? I thought you loved me.'

'I do. But…we haven't been lucky with marriage and wedding days. Do you think we could leave marriage till after we've had a couple of babies?'

'You want to have children *first*?'

'Mmm, yes. Do you mind?'

'Not at all. When do you want to start?'

He smiled at her, and she smiled back.

'Do those wonderful smiles mean what I think they mean?' his mother said as she rejoined them at the table. 'Could we be planning another wedding soon?'

''Fraid not, Mother dearest. Fiona wants to make you a grandmother before she makes you a mother-in-law.'

Kathryn looked surprised, then smiled herself. 'Really?'

'I'm a little superstitious,' Fiona explained sheepishly. 'Philip's been married twice already, and disasters come in threes.'

Kathryn nodded. 'I understand perfectly. And a marriage certificate is unimportant, really, so long as you really, truly love each other.'

'We really, truly love each other,' Philip repeated, and stood up. 'Which is why we're leaving. I want to show my house to the future mother of my children.

You did say you would like to live in Balmoral, didn't you?'

'I certainly did!' Fiona jumped to her feet, hardly believing the joy she was feeling.

'Bye, Kathryn.'

'Bye, Fiona, dear. Bye, son. Drive carefully.'

'Does this mean you want me to live with you?' Fiona asked him as he ushered her through the house and out to his car.

'But of course! Don't you want to?'

Fiona reached up to kiss him on the cheek. 'I want to more than anything else in the world.'

'So that's a yes?'

'Yes.'

'Great. We can start moving your things in today. Do you rent or own?'

'I'm paying off a unit.'

'Then sell it.'

'No, I'll rent it out,' she said, and he scowled.

'It's a good investment, Philip,' she insisted, then smiled. 'And a good place to stay if you ever get sick of me.'

'I'll never get sick of you.'

'You might. You don't know the new me all that well.'

'I *love* the new you.'

'Do you, now? Well, might I point out that the new me came here in her own car and she's going to drive it back?'

Again he scowled, and she felt a moment's worry.

'Philip…I'm not Noni any more. I have a career, and a mind of my own. And I won't be giving either up.'

'And you think I want that?'

'I don't know. Maybe.'

'I want *you*, Fiona. The you you are today.'

'Are you sure you don't mean the me I was last night?'

His smile was rueful. 'Her, too,' he said, and swept her into his arms. His kiss was long and hungry, yet at the same time tender and loving.

'I love you, Fiona Kirby,' he insisted afterwards as he held her close. 'I love your spirit of independence and your strength of character. I love your ambition and your commitment to perfection. I love your sophisticated beauty and your not-too-skinny body. And, yes, I admit it, I love the way you make love. But sex is only a part of what I feel for you. You must believe that.'

'Yes, Philip,' she agreed, her heart overflowing with love for him.

'God, when you say yes to me like that I just dissolve inside. Practise saying yes just like that, even when you don't mean it.'

'Yes, Philip,' she repeated huskily, and stretched up to kiss him on the mouth.

'Not *now*,' he protested. 'Later!'

'Yes, Philip.'

She said it later. A lot. And she finally said it five years later, to the question Philip had been asking her since their first child had been born.

Four-year-old Zachary and two-year-old Rebecca attended their parents' simple wedding ceremony on Balmoral Beach, their high spirits kept in line by their grandmother. Steve and his pretty new wife, Linda, were the two official witnesses.

Owen stood on the sidelines, trying not to complain

too much at the missed opportunity for Five-Star Weddings to shine once more at a Forsythe wedding.

'But she looks so beautiful in white,' he grumbled to Kathryn next to him. 'I wonder where she found that delicious dress. Do you know, I've never seen Fiona wear white before, let alone white chiffon.'

'I chose it for her,' Kathryn said, with a strange little smile.

'Really? Then you have excellent taste for bridal wear. You wouldn't be looking for a job, would you, Mrs Forsythe?'

Kathryn laughed. 'I have my work cut out for me looking after these little darlings two days a week, don't you think?'

'They're a handful, all right. But what can you expect with Philip and Fiona as parents? Talk about strong-willed! But they're a great match, aren't they?'

'Indeed they are. Shush, now, Owen, the big moment has arrived.'

The celebrant cleared his throat. 'Do you, Philip, take Fiona as your lawfully wedded wife, to love and to cherish, for richer for poorer, in sickness and in health, for as long as you both shall live?'

'I do,' Philip said strongly, and smiled warmly over at Fiona.

Fiona tried to smile back, but couldn't. She'd put this moment off for years. Not because she hadn't wanted to marry Philip, but because she'd been afraid, she supposed. Afraid of wedding days and wearing white and…and…

'And do you, Fiona,' the celebrant said firmly, 'take Philip as your lawfully wedded husband, for richer for poorer, in sickness and in health, for as long as you both shall live?'

She hesitated as the simple but beautiful vow sank in. Suddenly she realised what a coward she'd been, saying no to Philip's proposals all these years, being afraid to stand up and tell the world how much she loved this man, how she would love him till the end of her days.

What on earth was she afraid of? At thirty-three, she wasn't superstitious any more. She didn't believe in luck, or fate. She believed in forging one's own destiny, in actively choosing rather than letting things happen, in working hard and keeping faith with one's dreams.

For heaven's sake, she *wanted* to be Philip's wife more than anything else in the world. She always had. What was she waiting for?

'I certainly do,' she said, her smile dazzling.

Philip's handsome face burst into a wide smile. Their eyes met and they both kept smiling at each other as the celebrant said the all-important words.

'I now pronounce you man and wife!'

MILLS & BOON®

Next Month's Romance Titles

♡

Each month you can choose from a wide variety of romance novels from Mills & Boon®. Below are the new titles to look out for next month from the Presents...™ and Enchanted™ series.

Presents...™

A RELUCTANT MISTRESS	Robyn Donald
THE MARRIAGE RESOLUTION	Penny Jordan
THE FINAL SEDUCTION	Sharon Kendrick
THE REVENGE AFFAIR	Susan Napier
THE HIRED HUSBAND	Kate Walker
THE MILLIONAIRE AFFAIR	Sophie Weston
THE BABY VERDICT	Cathy Williams
THE IMPATIENT GROOM	Sara Wood

Enchanted™

THE DADDY DILEMMA	Kate Denton
AND MOTHER MAKES THREE	Liz Fielding
TO CLAIM A WIFE	Susan Fox
THE BABY WISH	Myrna Mackenzie
MARRYING A MILLIONAIRE	Laura Martin
THE HUSBAND CAMPAIGN	Barbara McMahon
TEMPTING A TYCOON	Leigh Michaels
MAIL-ORDER MARRIAGE	Margaret Way

On sale from 1st October 1999

H1 9909

Available at most branches of WH Smith, Tesco, Asda, Martins, Borders, Easons, Volume One/James Thin and most good paperback bookshops